My Piece of the Universe

AMARA ROMERO

DEDICATION

For you.

CONTENTS

ACKNOWLEDGMENTS

Thank you to everyone who contributed in one way or another to the production of this book. For production, my amazing editor Kya Francois and exctremely talented illustrater Freddie Spencer. For character developement, specifically Aliyah Romero, Maceo LIndsay, Kaelyn Peña, Tyler Basham, and Michael Krumland. Lastly, thank you to all of the english teachers who helped me realize my worth as an author by excluding me from socratic seminars.

1

"Um, hello, uh, is this Ch-child Protective Services?" I whispered into my phone, even though I was alone in my room, and I also already knew the answer.

"I need you to speak up, sweetheart." The lady on the other side replied, professionally, yet warm at the same time.

"Hi, uh, this is Child Protective Services, right?" I repeated, slightly louder, and stuttering less this time.

"Yes, why are you calling?"

"I would like to report my dad." I had rehearsed this conversation so many times in my head, and every time I had envisioned it, it had gone nothing like this. I didn't feel powerful like how I thought I would, I was just afraid.

"Okay. For what?" The lady seemed taken aback, this was not usually how Child Protective Services received cases.

"Um, I-" I started, and then I cut myself off. Maybe what he did wasn't bad enough, maybe this was all in my head like he told me. After a brief pause of consideration, I began to whisper again.

"I'm not sure if it's bad enough to report or not." I settled on.
"Darling, could you repeat that? You have to speak up."

"I'm sorry, um, I'm not sure if it's bad enough to report or not." There was a pause on the other side of the line.

"It's always better to be safe, so I'll connect you with a social worker. If it's not bad enough, nothing will happen. If it is, then we'll get you out of that situation." I breathed a sigh of relief.

"Um, okay, I-" I took a deep breath to calm my nerves. "Thank you."

"What's your name, sugar?" My heartbeat quickened.

"If I tell you my name, he won't know I'm the one calling? I mean, my dad won't know that it's me who called, right?" My voice hitched and my eyes began to water, not because I was sad, but because I was overwhelmed, and so, so afraid.

"Of course not, this is all confidential. What's your name?" After a brief pause, she added, "Take your time."

"T-Tuesday Ruiz." I stammered, after taking a moment to collect myself and reorganize my thoughts.

"And how old are you?"

"Fifteen."

"Alright, thank you. A social worker will call you in about ten or fifteen minutes from a different number, and keep an eye out for that. You are so brave."

"Thank you, uh, bye." I hung up.

The twelve minutes, I counted, in between the first call and the call with the social worker felt like ages. The sun shone through my windows, the glare making it hurt to look at my computer screen, I did it anyway. I ran my fingers down the sides of my phone, bits of glass from the broken screen poking into my fingers. It all made me feel so alive.

I would tell Venus about this later. Even though she sometimes claimed to enjoy going to our father's house, I knew it was all a facade to hurt our mother. Still, sometimes, I worry about how similar she is to him.

I had been planning on calling for five years, telling anyone who would listen about how horrible he is, my dad, I mean, but I wouldn't even go as far as to call him my father.

My mother and father had never meant to stay together, and they only got engaged after they found out my mother was pregnant, at eighteen, nonetheless. From what I've heard, her stepfather spent half the night interrogating him about what sort of father he would be. Not a very good one, it turns out. Sometimes I wonder why my mother didn't abort me, she would've been able to do so much more. She loved to travel, to see new places and meet new people, and in a way, she gave all of that up in order to have me, and I think she, well, sort of resents me for that. If I hadn't been born, she would've been able to stay wandering the world, going to parties, and waiting to find the right person to stay with. I think it could be my fault that I was stuck with my dad, but at the same time, I can't control whether I was born or not.

As I said earlier, the call from the social worker called twelve minutes after the other call ended.

"Hi, I'm calling to gather details on your case with Child Protective Services. What's your name?" She spoke with an accent that I could not place, her words blending together in a beautiful, yet difficult to understand tone.

"I already told the other lady," I said defiantly, masking my fear with confrontation, an unfortunate habit I developed from years of believing that emotions were, well, wrong.

"I'm sure you did, but I need your name, hun." She replied, keeping her voice strangely calm given my overreaction.

"Tuesday Ruiz, um, I'm sorry." I felt embarrassed.

"Alright. What are you reporting your father for?" I took a breath. My hands that were tightly gripping the edge of my bedsheet began to shake.

"Well, he locked me in my room once and-"

"When was this? How long were you there?"

"When did he lock me in the room?"

"Yes."

"It was about a month ago, and about a day." There was a silence at the other end of the line.

"What else?"

"He tried to kill me." A pause.

"What do you mean? How?"

"Once, we were driving, and we got into an argument about how diamonds were made, and I thought that it was joking at first. He was frustrated with me because I said that coal doesn't turn into diamonds. He got angry and pulled over the car and took me outside to yell at me. He pushed me against the car and had his hand around my neck, and it was really scary, and I- I couldn't breathe. I asked his girlfriend for help and she didn't help me, and it was really scary." All of this came out in a slurry while I was desperately trying to hide my stutter. I began to cry. Tear after tear came cascading down my face. I started having difficulty breathing even at the thought of what had happened.

"Tuesday, listen, you're safe now. You're going to be okay."

"And you aren't going to tell him that I was the one who called?"

"Of course not. What's your father's name?" I hesitated. What would her reaction be? She would know of the name for sure. "Tuesday? Are you still on the line?"

"Yeah, I'm here. His name is Raphael." There was a pause of what seemed like exasperation on the other end of the line, but I could've been making it all up in my head.

"Last name?"

"Ruiz. His name is Raphael Ruiz." There was a hesitation on her end of the line.

"And you're based in West Hills?"

"Yeah." She knew.

She asked a few more questions regarding my location and family, I talked about Venus, my mother, my father. She asked a lot of questions about my father. I'm not sure how many of those questions were really necessary to gather what was going on in our situation, and I had the awful feeling that this was going to go nowhere. My father was charismatic, rich, and most importantly of all, famous.

At a certain point, fame becomes more valuable than wealth. Global recognition trumps money, since having the world know your name is often worth quite a hefty price, a price that even money can't buy, and that was the price of fear.

My father was feared. Of course, he was admired, he was an unobtainable figure of charisma and charm, someone *just* out of reach for his fans who lived in West Hills. Maybe they would run into him in a grocery store, or pass him on the street. Perhaps they would even get a picture with him to post on social media. Everyone knows who he is.

But no one *really* knows who Raphael is, at least, not how he is inside. Not my mother, not Rowyn, not any of his fans. Gosh, I don't even think I know who he is completely. And now, this social worker, someone who I don't even know the name of, knows just a little bit about my father. Tears began to fall from my eyes once more, heavy drops that clouded my vision like cataracts.

"Tuesday? Are you still here? Did you hear me?"

"I'm sorry, could you repeat that?" I wiped the tears off of my face and glasses, composing myself.

"I just said that we will be making a visit soon, and to sit tight. I know that this is scary, and you're so brave for what you're doing, for you and your sister."

"Oh, thanks. Goodbye? Thank you." I had never been good on the phone.

"Goodbye. Be safe, and you're welcome." I hung up the phone.

I lied back onto my bed, feeling the effects of the lack of sleep I had been getting. I stared at the labeled glow in the dark stars I had stuck to my ceiling on my thirteenth birthday. I've always had a fascination with stars, nothing that I've ever considered pursuing, but I have star maps hung up in my room, and I'm always useful when you need to know if that one star you see is just a bright star or a planet, and I can almost always tell you what planet it is. So yes, the glow in the dark stars labeled in constellations and planets is just a little childish, but I don't have the heart to take them down. It was four in the afternoon. I went to sleep.

. . .

I woke up around eight in the evening. It had gone
dark, and the stars were revealing themselves,
though dimly. My mother would go to sleep in an
hour, then I would say hello to Venus and spend
most of my night on the roof. If I were lucky,
maybe Ellio would call me while I was up there,
and he would go outside, and we would look at the
stars together, talk about which stars were
particularly bright that night. I wanted to do my
homework, I had so many missing assignments I
had to do, but I could not get up. I could not make
myself get out of bed, and I felt awful about it. But
then, I couldn't do anything more than stare at my
ceiling, not even the things I loved, writing, singing,
or even getting up to go get a snack, that is, if my
mother wasn't in the kitchen.

Finally, I did get up, dragging my sore and
weak body out of the comfort of my room. I made
my way across the house, the cold, newly mopped
floor cold on my bare feet. My mother would have a
fit if she caught me walking without socks on the
clean floor, but she wouldn't. I don't even think she
was home.

My sister's room was, well, it could politely
be described as a mess. It was probably more
accurate to describe it as a landfill. Months, or
maybe even years, of clothing, garbage, and dishes
sat piled on every available surface. My mother
removed her doorknob because she kept locking her
door, so in the place of a lock, Venus stuck a tube of

chapstick, probably stolen, into the hole that the lock once was in. It was surprisingly effective, and impossible to get into her room without breaking either the door or chapstick, both very difficult to do. I knocked on her door.

"Venus, can I come in?" I bent over to look through the hole where her doorknob used to be.

"Yeah! One sec." I watched as she got off of the mattress that was in the corner of her room, surrounded by sugar-free Redbull energy drinks, to fiddle with the tube of chapstick. When she managed to get it out and open the door, I couldn't exactly move. Dishes were piled up to around my knees, with clothes and other pieces of trash covering the empty spaces between piles. It was near unlivable.

"Guess what I did?" I said, awkwardly stepping over and around the mess. Venus looked at me expectantly, one eyebrow raised. Once I had made my way to her mattress, I leaned over and whispered, even though we were alone in the house. "I called CPS on Raphael." Venus looked up at me, mouth agape. She was not the reactionary type, and this was not a reaction I expected from her.

Though she was two years and a half years younger, and I practically raised her, for a twelve-year-old, she acted and appeared to be my age, if not older. This had not always been the case though, and only really had been for the past few months. I was still getting used to strangers asking if we were twins, and them being shocked that she was not yet a teenager.

"Yes! Good job, Tuesday!" She said, clapping quietly. And though I was petrified of all that could happen to me because of this, I smiled. My stomach rumbled audibly. I had not yet eaten that day. "Let's get you something to eat before mom comes home, okay? I'll make you fried spam."

maybe we see different things
when we look at me
because maybe if i am really
as unhealthy as you describe,
i would see myself the way you did,
not worth of a plate at dinner

i'm bad
i know i'm bad
but with words twisted into knives,
so sharp they could cut the air
i wish you didn't remind me
quite so often

i'm afraid
they'll judge me like you do

i tell myself i love you
because i know that's what i'm meant to
but i can't love you
at least
not anymore

i carry the weight
of an unchosen side
and so i cut my hair
locks of femininity
that i did not choose
finally gone

who am i?
you make me wonder
how stupid do i have to be
to not even know myself

you make me question
if the sky is even blue

time has no meaning to me
because no matter how much
time i spent on you
you left eventually
like everyone else

how many times do i have to remind myself
that you don't care about me

the things i wish i could say,
i need help
i need to talk
i never will

2

I sat in the damp grass, my shadow elongated and disturbed, stretching across the land like a dark, eager arm. The seat of my suit pants was soaked with this morning's dew, which still clung to the grass, the trees, the flowers. The sprinkled drops of water shone in the light of the sun as it beamed down on the earth. It engulfed me in its painful warmth. Though it was autumn, the summer-like warmth touched everything. It rolled off the tips of the leaves, it snaked between the branches of the foliage of each tree and bush. Even the breeze seemed to be made of heat. I marveled, because even with the sun's burn so intense, the lingering dewdrops had not yet turned into steam.

I turned my head upward, as a sort of salute to the sky, allowing myself a deep, satisfying breath. The breeze tunneled across the open plain, whipping around my face as if it had made the journey for the sole purpose of caressing my face with its ghastly fingers, and kissing the reddened skin on my cheeks. It was the perfect place, I decided, to be alone, but not lonely, for I had the company of the trees, the wind, and the sky.

I hadn't been there for many years, for it had been many years since I needed to. Gael used to take Venus and me on walks up the trail leading here, and we all used to climb the very tree I was under. The climbing tree was a peculiar sight because unlike the other trees that stood upright all around it, the climbing tree seemed to be growing horizontally, like a stray piece of hair that simply will not stay put.

This field, this feeling, the ability to fill my lungs with the sky, these were a remedy that I had forgotten long ago. But today, old memories had resurfaced, and old pain was released in that torn photograph under my mattress, the one of my mother and father and me, a fake smile plastered onto my chubby, toddler face.

I stared blankly at my ink smudged fingertips, the stubborn black ink from the *Pride and Prejudice* ink set I stole from Barnes and Noble. Listening to the whispers of the wind and the birds that serenaded me from their hiding spots in the climbing tree, I pondered how long I had been sitting there, three hours, or twelve?

However long it was, it was long enough for the sun to swim from its position in the center of the sky, to now hang low over the horizon, making the clouds sag with heavy, golden light.

If I stayed all night maybe, I could watch as those clouds were wrung out like dishcloths, twisted in the dark until every last amber drop of light from the day was squeezed from them. Then, I promised, I would stay until morning, when the sun again spilled over the lip of the earth and filled the patient clouds with its light once more. And maybe then, I would stay until it came down again, bringing with it the memories of that day. Maybe then, I wouldn't ever have to leave.

Eventually, I did get up, the amber that once enveloped the sky stripped away as a sky as dark as my sister's jeans was painted over. I pulled my blazer around me tighter as I tightened my hand on one of the many protruding knots of the climbing tree, knots that made the tree so notoriously easy to climb. The rough bark made imprints on my hands as I climbed, the lines spelling memories of years of life and joy. That night, I remembered something that almost resembled the feeling of being carefree, the wind rustling my short hair into an indescribable mess as I hung upside down from one of the branches. As the blood rushed to my head, I couldn't help but wish that Venus was with me, or Ellio, or Claire, I just needed someone to share that night with.

And someone did come. I must have dozed off underneath the protection of the climbing tree, because I awoke to the sound of a loud engine, and to my dismay, driving right onto the field in a sleek, angular sports car, was my father and Rowyn. Rowyn was around twenty years younger than my father. When they started dating, she had just finished school, and he had an established career and two teenage children. She was nice and quiet, and she never seemed to have any opinions of her own. She seems almost completely aloof all of the time, and unaware of what was going on around her. I doubt she even knew that the relationship status in my father's social media description read "in an open relationship".

I sat up with a start, my entire backside soaked from the grass. I rubbed my eyes as the car pulled up next to me, headlights pointed directly into my eyes. I held up my hand in an attempt to block the blinding light, but it was no use. The only indication I had that my father was next to me was the sharp, numbing sting I felt across my face as his hand made contact with my cheek, and the scent of expensive cologne.

"Gorda, what the fuck are you doing out here?" He yelled, his tenor voice sending shockwaves through the field. I winced at my pet name, an apparently endearing way to call me fat. Before I could respond, it happened again, another slap on my already sore cheek.

"I'm sorry, Papa. I just fell asleep, I didn't mean to be out all night." My voice quavered, but I knew crying, well, showing any emotion, would make things so much worse for me. A kick to my ribs.

"Get in the car." He scoffed, turning around and making his way back. I obliged; how could I not?

The car ride back, though it couldn't have been more than two miles, felt almost as dangerous as what I knew was going to transpire the moment we got home. The car was riding the asphalt as a wave, the seemingly endless stretch of the hill that had not been paved over for years. The car, going at least ninety miles per hour on a windy, residential road, was a bullet with a target, and that target was me.

At that moment I wondered, would it be better if, as my father blindly whirled his car around those sharp turns my neighborhood was so notorious for, he forgot to turn the wheel, and Rowyn, Raphael, his sports car, and I, went hurtling into the side of a hill. Maybe Rowyn's or my father's airbags would save them, but in the back seat, I would get the worst of it. Maybe it would be worth it, though, for the chance of ridding the world of him. Wishful thinking. Raphael was like a cockroach, nothing could kill him.

As we neared his house, I prepared myself for what I knew was going to be hell. I had never been caught doing anything against the rules, the worst thing I had ever done before this incident was let Venus buy blue hair dye, and for that I was placed in solitary confinement, locked in the bedroom for almost a full day without my phone, or even a book. At my father's house, we didn't have designated rooms, just two bedrooms, and Venus and I always shared the monochromatic blue room at the end of the hall, only because the other bedroom's door didn't close right. That night, I ended up finding an old *Geronimo Stilton* book wedged between the dresser and the wall, and I ended up reading that one book twelve times. Venus was later sent into the bedroom to go to sleep, and we ended up talking for a bit before we fell asleep around six in the morning. I was still not allowed out when morning came. The hours dragged, and the silence felt deafeningly crushing. The blue felt deep and heavy, and the entire time I had the uneasy feeling one gets when they start to lose control of themselves while swimming. I was drowning in blue. When I was finally let out of the room, it seemed as though nothing had ever happened, and my father had forgotten about what I had done. This situation, as normal and simple as it sounds, really bothered me. I thought about it late at night when my terrors took over, my thoughts ravaging all rationality and logic. We never talked about it, and yet every time I hear my father close a door I wince. This time was different. No longer faced with the silence I had received last time, because this time, if I even dare say it, I actually did something to warrant severe punishment.

"Under pressure, coal turns into diamonds." I heard my father tell Rowyn, and though this was so clearly not true, the poor, oblivious person that was Rowyn marveled about how something so simple could turn into something so wonderful.

"I'm like that," He continued in his narcissism. "I was born into a poor family of immigrants and worked my way up, and look! Now I'm one of the only Mexican people in Woodbridge, living in a big house, in a career that I love." And sure, this could certainly be true, if drug dealing was the career that he loved.

Woodbridge was the area of the city that I lived in. It was known for being wealthy, pretentious, and most importantly, almost all white. I suppose my father took great pride in being one of the only not white people in our area, he brought it up in almost every conversation about his achievements, which, granted, with my father, were most conversations. Still, when asked where in our city I lived by classmates or teachers, my response usually warranted a response about how rich my family must be.

And then I felt the words slip out.

I didn't mean for them to, I had even been cautious of how loud I had been breathing. And yet, I could not stop my uncharacteristic hunger for always being right.

"Diamonds aren't made from coal." It felt like the air temperature dropped significantly, and goosebumps rise on my arms as I watched my father's charming smile fall into a frown.

"Yes. They are, Tuesday. I passed fifth grade." He said through gritted teeth, his hands gripping the steering wheel tighter.

"No, they aren't. You can look it up, Google is free." I had meant to stop. I could've just agreed and apologized, and everything would've been okay. Instead, though, Tuesday the idiot decided to continue.

The moment these fatal words had left my mouth, I knew things were going to be bad. Raphael pulled over and slammed on the breaks, causing Rowyn to grab the edge of her seat and my seatbelt to lock.

"Get out of the car. Out of the car!" He screamed, assuring all my neighbors knew exactly what was going on.

"Help me." I whispered to Rowyn as he stepped out to grab me. Tears involuntarily welled in my eyes as I felt my hands begin to shake. I balled them to make it less noticeable.

"Help me!" I repeated in a hiss, letting my panic show for just a moment. Rowyn stared back at me, her eyes displaying nothing more than the smallest sliver of fear, and probably for herself.

"Oh my god." She said, and nothing more. Raphael pulled me out of the car by my wrist, throwing me onto the asphalt.

"Get up! Who the fuck do you think you are?" I stood up, my knees turning to pudding beneath me. I didn't respond, but I got up and faced him.

My eyes were no longer welled with tears, he wanted a reaction, and I would not give him one. I took a breath, he shoved me against the trunk of the car. I did not wince.

"You are spoiled, stupid, rude, and disrespectful. You try to act all smart, but you know you aren't! You're a stupid fucking whore!" His hands were on my shoulders, fingers digging into my skin. It was going to bruise. I still didn't show a reaction.

And then, my father did something he hadn't ever done before. Whether it was rage or the fact that this time, without Venus here, he knew he could get away with it, because who would believe a fifteen-year-old over an adult? Moving one hand from my shoulder to my neck, he tightened his grip.

I soon fell to my knees due to the weakness I felt throughout my body, and yet, Raphael would not let go. As my father choked me, slowly, tormenting me, I noticed that the physical pain, no, it didn't hurt very much. What hurt was the betrayal, the invisible hand around my neck all of the time, choking invasive and awful thoughts into my head. I was never smart enough, never grateful enough, never modest enough. I hated myself.

It's okay to hate someone. It is. For when love goes into reverse, the result is hate, and that hate becomes a protective force. A force so powerful it blinds, obstructs our judgment, a spell that cannot be disbanded. Like my father. He hid his hate with gifts and money, but in the end, his love had failed him. There was no room in his heart for Venus and me, at least, not anymore. It was when my vision started to fail me, and my eyes began to cloud with darkness, that I finally gave in.

"Stop, please." I whimpered, barely audible.

"What'd you say to me, bitch?" His lips began to twist into a smile.

"Stop it, please," I said again, louder, my voice so hoarse I sounded four times my age.

"Why?" He asked, his smile growing larger.

"Because it hurts," I responded, my voice breaking from the effort it took to talk with his hand around my neck.

He threw me on the ground, and I gasped for air.

"Get back in the fucking car. I'm taking you to your mom's. I can't deal with you."

And I did.

maybe i'm afraid to be touched by anyone
because every time i feel hands near my neck
or cheek
or wrist
i always think it's you

like that time you poured gasoline
all over my favorite things,
and set them on fire
to watch me cry,

i have been gaslit.

one day,
you'll take your last
look at them.

and that's good,
i hope i already did.
because if i know i've already
seen you for the last time

maybe things will be okay.

i grew up,
and so you left.
the less i needed you,
the less you cared.

what i would give,
to have the wonders of a child,
once more

you said you just needed time
time away from me

but i gave you time
fifteen years of it, in fact
so why haven't you come back yet?

some people will never find true love.
and that's okay

love isn't for everyone

because some people,
no matter how much you love them
can never love you in return

dad?
i'm not feeling well
is it okay if i cry?

it won't be for very long,
don't worry

i want to be normal for christmas,
i told my mother when i was four
i want to have friends and toys,
and to feel
like the most loved child
to ever be

loving you shouldn't hurt
i was born to love you after all
and i guess i was born to be loved by you

but still,
the way you talk
they way you fold socks at me
whenever i mess up
tells me all i need to know about loving you

3

My hardwood floor felt sticky underneath me as I
awoke. I checked the alarm clock I had precariously
placed on my nightstand, it was four in the
afternoon, and my alarm had been quietly ringing
for the past four hours, when Claire and I decided to
take a nap after class, after staying up half the night
procrastinating chemistry homework and talking
about our lives. The room was aglow with delicate,
afternoon light, a warm energy that illuminated the
dust in the air. Though it was September, summer
heat leached out of the pores in the floor and the

walls. That week, it had consistently been over one hundred degrees, hot enough to melt my candles and break our air conditioning.

I turned my head and saw Claire asleep on the floor across the room, her pink hair stuck to her face, smudged eyeliner, and mascara still on her face from the night before.

Though I had only known Claire since the beginning of ninth grade, she was the closest friend I had. It wasn't like I had many friends, though. I tended to be sort of reserved and secluded, my social skills lacking severely. During the school year, she used to stay at my house for days on end, and since we began to quarantine, she stayed for weeks at a time. During that time, Claire would witness the sleepless nights I would spend, clutching my phone, my hand clamped so tightly over my mouth so I would not make a sound.

Things have gotten better recently, he hasn't been bothering me as much, and since things fizzled, he doesn't get as mad at me if I go to sleep earlier than usual. Things were definitely getting better. Maybe, someday soon, I would have the courage to leave for good.

I then realized the reason I had woken up. My usually energetic, aggressive even, mother, was knocking timidly at the half-open door. I sat up, looking down, avoiding eye contact.

"Tuesday?" She said softly, whispering, almost. "Child Protective Services is here."

At this point, Claire had woken up, and without a word, or thought, I was suddenly wide awake. I patted my hair down and grabbed a mask with my free hand. I walked into my backyard without shoes on, the ground was warm.

"Hello, Tuesday Ruiz?" She said to me through her mask with an embroidered unicorn on it. It didn't quite fit her face right, gapping at holes around her mouth and nose, so I wasn't quite sure it was really doing anything. I nodded.

She was wearing suede, high heeled boots. She stood, leaning on one leg and popping the other out in a pose. My mother rushed out after me to pull up a chair for the lady, and she sat down with a clipboard in hand. My mother stood expectantly yet cautiously, waiting for the lady to speak.

"Gael Jacobs?" She addressed my mother.

"Yes. Is there anything I should do?" My mother stood awkwardly, awaiting further instruction.

"I'm going to speak to Tuesday for a little bit, and then to Venus, and then I'll speak to you." My mother went back inside, I pulled up a chair for myself.

"Your father Raphael Ruiz? Let's start with the accusations."

"Okay."

"So it says here that he locked you in a room for about a day, is that true?"

"Yes," I said confidently and surprisingly, loud enough to hear, though my heart was pounding and my hands were shaking.

"And that he tried to..." She trailed off, probably looking for a more professional, more emotionally detached way to say it. "He tried to asphyxiate you?"

"Yeah."

"I'm so sorry, you are so strong." And that's what they all said. Every therapist, every friend I had opened up to in the past about my abuse. I suppose that's for a reason, though. Abuse is something we read about on the news, something we hear about in cautionary tales from our parents, but never something we expect our friends to go through, right under our noses. "I just have a few more questions for you, Tuesday."

"Okay, um, what are they?" I said through broken breaths, my hands tightly clasping onto the armrests of my chair.

There are things I wished people had noticed, like the one day I came to school with a bruise surrounding my eye and nose, or that time during French class when silent tears began to fall while we were watching a movie that depicted domestic violence. I wish I had been brave enough back then to tell Claire, to tell a teacher, *I'm being abused, help me*, but I never was. It's difficult, admitting that someone you love so much can be so, so evil.

The term 'evil' is far too subjective to really mean a single thing to everyone, and really, I'm skeptical of it really meaning anything at all. But there is one thing I know about evility, and that one thing is that Hunter was evil.

I think that for me, the line is when one does something, for no other reason, other than to hurt someone, that is evil. When what you're doing does absolutely nothing other than hurt someone, you're not gaining anything from it, but getting pleasure and happiness from the pain and suffering of others, that's what it means to be evil. And Hunter was. Sure, he did things that benefited him plenty, but so much of what he did, so much of what he put me through, had no purpose other than to make me hurt, and to watch as I slowly slipped away into a mindless, brainwashed, empty shell of what I used to be.

It started with the rules. No makeup out of the house, and if I wore it to school? I would get cheated on. No crop tops, no dresses, no shorts, no skirts. And nothing tight fitting. What would've happened if I had done these things? What was normal for me to go through during this painful period of my life could be, to others, considered psychological torture.

"You make me want to shoot myself in the brain." He said in a text message one time. "Every single time you talk to another boy, you make me want to kill myself." He would say. It didn't matter, in our relationship, that he cheated on me, almost weekly, according to him. I wasn't allowed to have rules for him, because that would've been abusive. He broke up with me a few times, once because I came out to him, as queer. That one was the most memorable.

*"So you're a f*g now, huh?" He said after I told him, angry in his homophobia.*

"I'm not, I'm so sorry, I just got confused, that's all. I'm straight, I promise. I'm sorry I was just overthinking."
"What were you thinking about? You've had sleepovers with Claire, you've been in the same room as her."

This sort of conversation had been going on for the hours after I came out, berating me, making me lose my drive to argue. What I didn't mention here was that he had cheated on me, asked out other people, so sleeping in the same room as my best friend really shouldn't have been anything for him to worry about.

And yet, there were worse things. Things so terrible, I would cry thinking anyone but myself, and maybe Claire, knew what had happened to me. Even I hadn't come to terms with what had happened to me, not until very recently. Some things, some terrible, miserable things, are better kept hidden away, so people who care about the person hurt don't feel any sort of pain, and don't have to worry, at least, that's how I felt.

This feeling, again, connected to a larger issue. Failure to reach out, failure to ask for help, and a fear of all these things, a fear of failure. The paradoxical, incessant cycle that continued to rob my head of free space, and make it impossible to let anyone know what was going on. *Things are good!* I would say, *Hunter and I are great!* I would tell if anyone asked. If I had just stopped for a moment, pushed aside the fear and failure and fear and failure that clogged my head, and said I needed help, this could've been over so much sooner.

"Has your mom ever done anything that hurt you?" The child protective services lady said. I was taken aback. This was supposed to be about my dad, not about my mom.

"Um, maybe? No. No, she hasn't." In my confusion, I said something wrong. Something very, very wrong. The lady looked up from her clipboard to look me directly in the eyes. She set her pen down, she crossed her arms.

"You need to tell me the truth, Tuesday." And it seemed like she actually cared.

"No, not like my dad," I said, and this was the truth. My mother hurt me in other ways, but nothing that could be classified as abuse, right? Two people had done that to me, and my mom was so much lesser than them.

"Has she hurt you in other ways? Like verbally, or emotionally?" I was quiet. I began to think. Could my mom also be evil? My savior, the person who pushed so hard to get me away from my dad.

"A little." I settled on.

"How?"

"Sometimes, when she thinks I'm looking fat, after I eat, she'll give me things to make me throw up, or just not let me eat or eat very much." The woman looked appalled. She dropped her composure, she was not prepared for this kind of answer.

"I'm sorry, I'm really sorry, I don't know what to say."

"Yeah." She looked at the ground.

"Yeah."

Then she called Venus out, and I went back inside, straight to the shower, and just, got in. Showering with clothes on is strangely therapeutic, the physical feeling of heaviness of my soaking clothes weighing me down, drowning out the heaviness in the air, comforting. I lied down. I was tired, tired of lying, tired of thinking about what would happen if I finally told the truth. I eventually returned to my room, too desensitized and numb to convey any feeling, any speculation, or really hold any real conversation with Claire. I just sat on my bed, staring at nothing.

"Tuesday?" Claire asked after some time had passed. I looked up at her. "Are you okay? What happened?"

"Yeah! I'm okay, and nothing really, they just asked questions. We should really get started on that chemistry homework soo." I said with a laugh. I was usually good at things school-related, but because of the volume of the work I was assigned in chemistry as such a vulnerable time in my life, it was hard to keep up. Due to my overwhelming fear of failure, though, I maintained a low A, but sometimes it would dip to a high B, and I hated this. Sometimes, though, no matter how hard I tried, no matter how long I stared at my blank notebook, I simply could not get the motivation to pick up a pen and start to do my homework, even if it was relatively easy.

About two hours into our pursuit of absolutely nothing, we gave up. We sang karaoke and danced, watched sappy reality TV shows about people who we wouldn't care about in the morning, but were so invested in that moment. I must have noticed, somewhere, that we hadn't eaten lunch or dinner that day, and for some reason, I was okay with that. It had gotten late, the rest of my family was asleep, and I had come to the realization that I needed to do my chemistry homework.

"Claire, we should actually do the homework now." We were lying on my floor, lights off, candles lit, and music blasting.

"Yeah, probably." We didn't move.

"Hey, what if we do the homework drunk? I doubt he'll check for accuracy." I said with a smile. We got up.

My mom wasn't a big drinker, but she kept quite a bit of liquor, at least twenty half-empty bottles in the cabinet above the fridge. Claire and I poured two glasses half full and filled the rest with coffee, it was disgusting. We ran back to my room snickering and laughing and chugged the rest sitting down on my bedroom floor.

"Tuesday?" She slurred after a while.

"Yeah...?" I replied, equally, if not more slurred.

"You should text *Ellio!*" She said a bit too loudly. I hushed her.

"O-okay Claire... but only! If you..." I smirked. "Text Caleb!" She mockingly gasped.

"A deal's a deal."

Ellio was brilliant and beautiful, both everything I wished to be and everything I wished for in a partner. We had been dating for roughly two weeks at this point, and he already was a huge part of my world and life, and I loved him, more than words can possibly convey. *I love you more than Harry Potter. I promise.* I typed out and hit send.

"Claire, are you crazy? It's three in the morning!" I yelled.
"Too loud, too loud." She responded, and that's about where my memory stopped for that night. My memory came back about midway through doing the chemistry homework, and surprisingly, I wasn't doing too terribly. I checked my phone, and even though it was only shortly after five in the morning, Ellio had responded. *Of course I'll marry you, dummy.* He responded. I couldn't help but smile.

I dragged myself through my classes, fighting off a horrible hangover with the incumbent stress that I was still not used to at this point in my life. Honestly, I really don't remember much. I know that I went to the park with Claire and Ellio, I know that Ellio and I got into a fight and that we ran into Caleb there on purpose. I remember coming home, determined to go the rest of the day without food. I felt so ugly, so fat, just, so bad. And I remember my mom picking up Japanese food, with the reminder for me to not eat too much, I was already getting fat. I remember getting in bed, feeling like my world was going to collapse, and then I remember standing up, and then waking up on the floor, Claire shaking me.

"Let's go get you some food, okay?" I began to cry.

"Okay."

i apologize, to my body
i'm sorry i don't appreciate
all the things you do for me

and instead i hurt you

every moment
of every day
constantly telling you,
you're not good enough.

i'm so afraid of failing,
i hardly ever try,
but when i start to cry it rains,
so i look up to the sky,

and i pray to god,
a god, who supposedly hates me,
for who i am and who i love,
god, please

i'm waiting for that day,
when we've grown up
and we know better

and you can say,
with sincerity,
i'm sorry

The world feels heavy like an old TV
The shoes I'm wearing are falling apart
It's light outside but I can barely see
I'm not happy I wish life could restart
If something changed I really can not be
The taste of bubblegum stays on my tongue
And so does the smell of a popsicle
Though it has been years since I have felt young
The trope of age feels paradoxical
Time to leave now, I want to go home
Away from this vast, bleak world I will roam

you deprived me of a childhood
i was adult at 10
and yes that's bad, and yes you're bad,
but you can make me pasta

everything i thought good about myself
you made me hate
you are the only person i know,
to make good things turn bad in just an instant

i like this shirt
i'm sorry, i don't
i didn't mean to lie like that
but maybe if you weren't around
i would like it

maybe i can leave
if you find somebody new
you might cut the strings
around my wings
and at last bid me adieu

i hate you
i hate you for what you did to me
because i never thought,
that someone could make me hate myself
as much as i hated you

i'm sorry,
not to you, but to myself
for allowing myself to get caught up with you

4

It was hot again, hot enough to coax me out of a wool sweater and into a cropped shirt. I still kept my blazer hung over my arm as I walked from where my mother dropped me off to a nearby bench.

"Hey!" Ellio jogged over to me, phone in hand.

"Hi!" I said back, and we began to walk, hands so close to being linked, but not.

The way I felt about Ellio was unlike how I felt about anyone else, and I could talk about it forever. Yes, it was the normal, typical school crush, but to me, it was more. I was so transfixed by him, so starstruck, that I could not mess up.

Over the phone the other day, I offered to bring him one of the two copies of the book I had written. He had seemed so thrilled and really excited to read it, despite confessing to me just moments before that he hadn't read a book for pleasure in at least the past year. He listened to me laugh as I decorated it with stickers and drawings, writing a note in the back of it.

You're perfect. I had written. *I'm so glad I met you.* And I meant it.

And a letter. It spanned about a third of a sheet of lined paper, it was brief. I talked about how much I cared about him, and in what way I did. I didn't end up putting it in between the pages of the book like I had planned but instead kept it tucked away in my pocket as we walked along the sidewalk, just in case I changed my mind or felt bold that day. We walked until we found a big, grassy field, and we sat down. The conversation flowed so easily, I couldn't stop looking at him, and I could tell how my face was growing red, I seemed awkward, and so I lied down in the grass.

"The bees are my friends," I said, barely thinking about the words coming out of my mouth. Yes, it was stupid, and I probably should've thought about something a little less dumb to say, but that's just how it was around Ellio. I loved him so much he made me forget about everything I had rehearsed to say, everything that I had thought out. I was just completely, truly myself around him, it was safe.

"Oh really?" He said with a laugh, and I could feel the smirk on his face. I smiled.
"Yes, this one is named Jessica." I immediately cringed, but Ellio laughed, and I forgot about worry. I continued to ramble, probably for several minutes, about the bees. Their names, what their lives were like. He just had that effect on me, the giddiness of having a crush making me forget all order and logic.
"I'm sorry, that was dumb," I said lightheartedly, a smile on my face. Ellio's face came into view beside me, he had also lied down.

"No, it was nice." He said, staring at me, his pale eyes of a color that I could not place staring into mine.

By the time I left, Ellio didn't know, but I had fallen deeply in love with him that day. He made me feel that kind of safety and warmth that I had longed to feel with Hunter, even pretended was there.

That night, Ellio and I stayed up on the phone until almost three in the morning. We had plans to sneak out that night, but Ellio got tired, so he ended up going to sleep. I stayed up for hours after, watching the sky lighten from a navy, blue as the melancholy sky, and soon, a sky like forget-me-nots dominated my world. Though I could feel the exhaustion seeping from the seams of my very being, my mind was so awake with daydreams, daydreams too wonderful to simply end by falling asleep.

But eventually, when the sun shone so brightly through my circular windows I was forced to close my eyes, I drifted off. I don't remember exactly what I dreamt that night, but when I woke up just after noon, I was drenched in a cold sweat, and tears immediately came to my eyes. I sat up, short of breath as my room and the world around me seemed to be crumbling, breaking, as my body cried for sleep. I stumbled to my bookshelf, where just a drop of water was left in a glass from the night before, but it was enough. I lied down on my cold, hardwood floor, letting the heat from my body travel down, down into the cold floor, into the earth. My back was sore from the slouch I'd developed from constantly carrying bags too heavy, and seemingly carrying the weight and stability of my broken family. I crawled over to my dresser, reached into the bottom drawer that I kept my sweaters in, and found a flask. I sat up and drank half of it in a single sip. I glanced at the clock, it was one in the afternoon. I wanted to hit myself, why couldn't I stop?

Ten minutes later, though, I was happy. The universe seemed blurrier, the bits that hurt me and caused pain glossy, glossed over, so blurry I could not make them out. I reached for my phone. I texted Ellio.

I'm really drunk. I wrote, the simple sentence laden with typos.

Tuesday, how'd that happen :(. He responded, and I called him.

"Ellio!" I nearly yelled.
"Tuesday, too loud." He shushed me.
But I don't remember much of the rest of that day. My mother was out again that afternoon and evening, and probably most of the night. All I can remember is the bubbly happiness, the kind of addictive joy that makes all other joys pale in comparison. To have the ability to smile and laugh until every last drop of pain was wiped up by the mop that was liquor.
Eventually, I sobered, though, and I texted Ellio again.

Hey, sorry about earlier. I wrote.

Don't worry about it, I'm glad you're sober now. Call? He responded immediately.

Of course. I wrote back. I called him.

Like calls with Ellio tended to go, we were on the phone for hours. The way I could talk to him forever and never get bored, or run out of things to talk about, or the way he engulfed my entire universe in just a week, was all unmatched. Ellio meant the world to me, if only I was brave enough to tell him exactly how much that was.

"Tuesday?" He said.

"Ellio?" I responded, he smiled.

"We aren't socks but I think we'd make a good couple." He said. I laughed, we had been going over pick up lines the light before. "I mean, we aren't socks but I think we'd make a good pair!" He said, and I laughed even harder.

We continued our conversation as usual, but I couldn't help notice how my cheeks had grown hot at the random use of a pick-up line. That was just Ellio, though. Completely ridiculous, completely insane, completely perfect.

"Tuesday?" He said again after a bit.

"Yes?" I said this time.

"I was serious about that pick-up line earlier."

"Really? Maybe you're just tired, do you really like me or are you just tired?"

"I like you. Do you?"

"I do, but wait."

"Yeah?" I laughed.

"Okay, so, this might sound a little bit stupid," I said, and he gave me a strange look. "So it's past midnight on September eighth," I continued, Ellio laughed.

"Uh-huh..."

"So ask me out tomorrow because it's September ninth, so in writing, it will be 9/9, which is prettier than 9/8." We both laughed, my irrational obsession with dates being showcased once again. "Alright, Tuesday." He looked at me, and the look in his eyes is something that I will never forget.

Ellio went to sleep, and I was happy. Not the same kind of happiness I got from drinking, where all the suffering was glossed over like they didn't exist, but the kind of happiness that makes the pain not matter, nothing seemed to matter, as long as I got to be with Ellio, and I got to see him and talk to him every day, knowing that, unbelievably, yet, so wonderfully, someone as lovely and as perfect as Ellio, well, loved me.

I went to sleep. The morning came fast.

Coincidentally, September ninth is now known for being the day that the sun never came up. Smoke from wildfires that raged, dominating the skies all along the California coast. I think assuming the sun never came up that day was easy, the sky all day was dark, covered by a dark, orange-yellow mass of smoke. But, the sun did come up. The sun always comes up, but sometimes it's covered, like September ninth. That day, my universe revolved around Ellio, like he was my sun, the thing that lit up the world when it got dark. Yeah, Ellio was the sun.

I couldn't tell my parents. My mom was already suspicious, because even though I was most definitely queer, any boy who I spent time around was automatically my boyfriend, to my mother. Frustrating as it was, she was right with Ellio, and since I had spent so much time giving her the "girls and boys can just be friends" lecture about a week before, she would've lost her mind, and really, that's okay. She didn't need to know everything about my personal life, not that she really cared anyway.

Though school was strange, and the darkened sky made time feel off, September ninth is a day that I will remember for the rest of my life. I called Ellio after school. We discussed how strange and odd everything felt that day and other serious topics before he just stopped talking, and looked at me with a smile.

"What are you looking at me like *that* for?" I said jokingly, a half-smirk plastered across my face.

"Would it be bad if I said something?" He said, vaguely.

"Said what?"

"That, maybe I'm just in the moment, but I might love you, I think. I know it's only been like, a day so you can break up with me if you want." He said with a smirk, knowing full well that I was not going to break up with him.

"Well, guess what, dummy?"

"What?"

"I love you, Ellio."

"I love you, Tuesday."

"I know," I said, and we both laughed.

I was overflowing with happiness until dinner time. Venus even asked why I was smiling so much, but I didn't tell her. For now, it was mine and Ellio's secret, and that made it special.

Dinner was not happy. My mom actually cooked for once and made us sit down and pretend like we were a normal family. I sat stiffly beside my mother and across from my sister, the family portrait from years ago still on the mantle, laughing at us, the sick, twisted mockery of what a family was meant to be.

"Tuesday, don't eat so much, you've already gained so much weight in the past few months." Yes, I wanted to say. Yes I have, and now I'm at a normal, healthy weight for my height, but instead, I didn't say anything. With Gael, I had to pick and choose my battles, and this was one that, no matter how hard I pushed, and no matter how many facts I presented her with, I would not win.

And losing is okay sometimes, it isn't possible to win every single thing we set out to do. Ellio didn't know yet, he didn't know about how bad my family really was. He was at dinner with his, and he was happy enough with his family that I didn't feel the need to burden him with my troubled existence any further. Besides, he was already dating me.

That was a problem I had, always feeling like I was bothering people by just my existence, and that just by extension of knowing me, people around me were burdened and unfortunate. I know now that this usually isn't true, and most of the people who are my friends, or close to me at all are there because they choose to be, not because of pity, or moral obligation like I had thought for so many years.

The food. I looked to Venus, who looked disgusted, but not surprised about what Gael had just told me, and I looked to my mom, the mom that I wished had cared about me, her expectancy, how she was waiting, and I gave up. I realized I couldn't do it. I couldn't do this anymore, this constant fight with her, the constant battle I dealt with every day, my mom demanding complete control over what I ate and how I looked, and I realized in that moment, I had no choice but to give in, I couldn't win this one. I knew it, Gael knew it, and Venus, bless her heart, even she knew it.

So I emptied my plate into the trash.

i know,
that when the story of my life is over,
no more pages left to turn and run over,
the chapters which include you,
will be the loveliest.

just fun at first so sharp and fragrant
i crave and crave my entertainment
and to the worlds and my amazement
that joy i get has no replacement

i can't get the thoughts
clear in my head
i had too much to drink
and now i want to go to bed

no
tonight i won't let
the night infect me
i can forget
i know i can forget
let me forget

what's in a name?
what's in a swing?
the power to make me flinch
at least,
if it's coming from you

i wish we never met
not because i don't love you
more than the moon
and more than the stars,
but because if we never met,
i wouldn't have ever known
that you were my weakness

in a sea of darkness
you were my light
until i got closer,
and i realized
you were a fire
ravaging
destroying my world
until the only thing left
was
you

why won't you stop

they tell you about it in school
you hear it on the news
how it destroys people
how it destroyed me
but there's so much they don't tell you
like how you don't even fight back,
you're just numb
and frozen
and stuck
oh,
so stuck

i wish i had the power
to control
what they do
to me

5

I am alone in this moment of peace. This moment of still, this moment of being, I ask, will the sun come up today? Will the rain wash all the pain away? The night is tranquility, by grace of medicinal modernities traded for crisp night air, and I'm living. I know that I'm living tonight, for the earth is warm and the wind is cold, and age feels inevitable, like a chore we must complete, and I ask again, why must we grow old, as the earth is just beginning it's life?

And then I think of you again, and what you did to me, how you made me hate myself and my body every time you hit send on your worn-out flip phone.

And it's summer, it's July, it was your sixteenth birthday, and the last time I saw you. That was the excuse you used too. How could I possibly be angry with you, for all the misery you put me through, if it was your birthday?

Ironically enough, that was also the day I realized I didn't love you anymore. I hadn't really for months, and it had been months since we had seen each other, but the kind of dependency you gain from being so close to someone for such a shockingly large part of your adolescence is unmatched.

And then I woke up in tears, it was five in the morning. This was the problem with going to sleep so early, the night terrorized me as I slept. I held my head between my hands, rocking back and forth. My joints felt gummy, the air dry and heavy. As I lied back down I affirmed myself, *I got away, I'm safe, I'm with Ellio now, and Ellio is good to me. It's been months. It's safe. It's been months.*

He knows where you live. I finally thought, and the cycle started over, that was the last straw. I didn't get back to sleep that night.

If I'm being honest, before we met, I didn't have any plans of living past twenty-five. I figured that I would peak sometime in my late teens or early twenties, and from that point on, it would be a meteoric downfall, hopes and dreams being cast aside and done with. But things changed, and suddenly, the meteoric downfall I had been planning all my life was suddenly replaced with daydreams of all the time I could spend with you, and all the things I could experience with you, past twenty-five.

And I realized, I love you. I love that you're safe, and how you make the ticking time bomb of life seem beautiful. I've always been a writer, yet my novels and short stories had never been short of bittersweet. The melancholic undertones of all my writings reflecting the inner torment I subjected myself to. When I was younger, I developed a metaphor, a short story I called "The Man in the Meadow." I didn't know what I was writing at the time, I didn't know that the story, and the character, was based on how I felt at the time, a longing, a lust, to die a beautiful, metaphorical, remembered, death.

I grew invested in the man, I submitted the story as an assignment in my Creative Writing class, and the feedback I got was, well, not what I had expected. I held this story so incredibly close to my heart, any subjection of criticism absolutely ruined me. When my teacher told me it made no sense, it was just philosophical ramblings disguised as a story, convoluted, even, I couldn't handle it. A year later, I reworked it, and though my teacher probably would've found it even more difficult to follow, it was perfect in my eyes. And the story went a little like this:

As time passes and people come and go, some are able to cope with the inevitable rise and fall of their generation, and themselves. They are able to know that someday, they will be meaningless to a world that values material and trivial things over the remembrance of human life. However, this was not the case for the man in the meadow.

Society praises celebrities and world-changers years after they've departed. The time-old tale of heroes and villains, both remembered and kept on the forefront of minds, why? Why, well, because they've made real impacts on the lives of hundreds. Villains and Heroes are the ones who are remembered, the ones we think about bored late at night, no matter what the narrative. It's awfully hard to remember every single background character, the characters who may never even be mentioned. Given this, some are left to wonder, if life is simply another story, who are these so-called "background characters" in our society?

The man in the meadow was considered odd by the townspeople who lurked in the villages above him. They would watch and gossip about the man as he lay in the meadow, watching the sky spin and talking to himself. The man was far past his prime, a veteran university drop out who had worked a mediocre job before retiring at a normal age. Mediocre and average in all senses, the man really was a background character in the story of life.

The meadow was on the edge of the quaint farming town he had lived in all his life. The townspeople often steered away from the meadow, worrying about the bugs and grime that often comes with vast fields of flowers and assorted flora.

Many of the children in town were fascinated by the man who spent all of his time in the meadow, far from any sort of civilization. These children eventually grew out of their curiosity and grew up. They left, something the man could never bring himself to do. University was one thing, but he really didn't last very long. Children grow up, teenagers aren't ever good for much, and adults grow old and die. And so, the children who once marveled over the man were all gone in spirit now, the curiosity was gone forever.

However, there was one child, out of the dozens who became infatuated with the man, whose curiosity did not dwindle as he made his way into his teenage years. The boy was only six years old when he had noticed the man whilst he was on a walk with his mother. He was at first enchanted by the brilliance of the picturesque meadow, with hundreds, if not thousands of beautiful flowers and florets, creating a boundless sea made up of color and beauty. Perhaps an anthophile, the man would lie in the meadow for hours, surrounded by the aroma of thousands of blooms, and staring into the sun. This perplexed the boy, and soon, they each had earned a friend in one another.

This strange and unlikely friendship blossomed from a mutual respect of each other's lifestyles. Who are children to judge, anyway? Before being educated, they are more often than not exact replicas of their parents and their parent's beliefs. Aside from this, the man was not exactly in a place to judge, either. A small child and a man who has chosen to outcast himself from both community and companionship, an unlikely pair, but it worked, somehow, and the two formed a bond unlike any other.

As a background character, meeting and befriending the boy was in all likelihood the highlight and pivotal point of his, in all other aspects, middle of the road and ordinary life. Unfortunately for the man, this only gave the townspeople more to gossip about. Comments of grooming and preying on the young boy were not uncommon for the man to fall victim to. While most on the receiving end would scoff at and deride these claims, the man just didn't hold with such nonsense. The man simply would not address the situation, because due to his isolation from the community, the lonely man learned to never talk, which only furthered the outrageous claims of which the people fabricated, day after day.

The man had never been the subject of any hate or ridicule until he had grown old. Something that came with age, the sense of inferiority from American society. This sort of treatment was not something the man was exempt from, and the animosity and ageism only began to worsen as he grew older and as his life began to wane. The man was now obsolete, and with the ever-present thought of death looming over him, the man was filled with a feeling of dread, and it was not going to be leaving him until he was gone.

Considering how odd and strangely introspective this man was, it would seem increasingly uncommon for him to be of any interest to children after they've been groomed to like the trivial aspects of life by society. For a young child, a man who does nothing but lie in a meadow all day is all but the most entertaining thing in their confined idea and view of the universe. As they grow older, though, this view broadens into something where the word "fascinating" no longer encapsulates the man. This was the case for every child but the boy, the main character of the story of life, at least in the point of view that contains these two fundamental characters, but not the main character of my story. Of course, the role of the boy is crucial to the story of the man, but this begs the question; is crucial necessarily, well, necessary?

The meadow was filled with a sweet, delicate odor, quite like the perfume that the man's mother had worn. The wildflowers gave off a scent similar to lavender on a warm spring summer day, and the few houses near to the meadow often kept their windows and doors ajar, and when the warm wind ever so often blew in through the windows and doors, the lavender-like scent wafted through, blowing their thin curtains every which way.

The meadow was the epitome of beauty, however, the people in the town entirely disliked its presence. Perhaps it was jealousy, as no human being can possibly be as prepossessing as a congregation of flowers, or, perhaps it was the man, a predominant figure in the meadow, arguably obstructing its beauty.

Beauty is in the eye of the beholder, and even if the town thought the meadow was an obstruction of it, the man was in love with the beauty of the meadow. There is something about colors and meadows that are simply pleasant to the eye. Especially in the spring and summer, the colors mixed into a melting pot of beauty and untouched alacrity, a beautiful mess.

A beautiful mess.

Wasn't that all that life was, after all? The mess part, absolutely, was all I used to see life as. Random splotches of paint, splattered at random across our bleak world, painting people, monsters, lovers, you. But beautiful, the concept of everything being a *beautiful* mess was completely unknown to me, until I met you. The random splotches were art, the monsters were misguided, the lovers were blessed, and you? You were just, well, you. And that was perfect. That was more than perfect, more than enough, more than I could've ever asked for, or dreamed of. Everything you did made sense, it made sense of the mess of the world, and made it beautiful.

I was getting ready to see you, we were going to the park. Maybe we would get coffee, childishly trying to pay for it before the other. It didn't matter what we did or didn't do, all that mattered was that you were you, and I couldn't wait to see you.

It was suffocatingly hot, again. It was October, and still not cooling down. How I longed for the rain to wash the cars parked along my street and water the flowers I had planted in my garden months ago. It was nearing Halloween, and I was yet to choose a costume. I hadn't dressed up the year before, Claire and Hunter had dragged me to a house party, where the guests were all disgustingly intoxicated and scary. This was the only party I had ever been to. I had never done well around people, something Hunter had always failed to understand. Claire was better about it, she never made me do anything I was strictly opposed or uncomfortable with. Needless to say, that night was the worst. Whether it was Hunter cheating on me, or accusing me of cheating with his best friend because I laughed at one of his jokes, it was miserable. Hunter called me a whore because of that incident until the day I ended things.

Ellio and I walked, hands intertwined, under the scorching sun up to a bridge. The path to get to the landing underneath the bridge was steep, almost a direct incline. It was beautiful too, the grey concrete that made up the bulk of the bridge was covered in spray painted pictures of everything imaginable, messy, yet beautiful. We began our ascent.

Not even halfway up, I knew something was wrong. It used to happen on roller coasters, where black splotches cover my vision completely, and I am taken with dizziness. I collapsed against a pillar of the bridge. Ellio was significantly ahead of me, so it took him a moment to realize that I had fallen. He ran back down.

"Tuesday, are you okay? What's wrong?" I couldn't speak, I couldn't tell him that this was what happened when I didn't eat for too long. "Is this okay?" He asked as he gingerly put his hand on my back. I nodded and leaned into him.
And we sat there for a while. I eventually told him that we should probably get something to eat, or drink, and then we could continue our walk. We did.

I was about to be picked up when my mother called me.

"That's strange." I wondered aloud.

"What is?"

"My mom is calling me." For a normal person my age, this might not have been something to be worried about, but my mother had always made a point to never call me, no matter the circumstance, unless I was in serious trouble. And last time I checked, I had hidden my flask and cigarettes well. I answered the phone.

"CPS visited Raphael today," I stopped walking, my vision clouding over. "They're recommending that, for your safety, you spend a few days away, and then," I could hear her collecting herself on the other end of the line, but that was impossible, my mother never cried. "They're putting you and Venus in foster care." I couldn't respond, my vocal chords twisting and tying themselves into bows and knots in my throat, but that didn't matter. My mom hung up the phone.

"What was that?" Ellio asked, innocently. I threw myself into his arms.

i miss it
back when it was first
back when it was a mistake
But first turned to seventh
And mistake turned into
you're not good enough
and i can't control myself

why is it over
why does it have to be over
why does it need to be over
why isn't it over yet?

goodbye house
goodbye room
goodbye everyone
goodbye to you

but how long will goodbye last?
a moment or forever?
i'd prefer to keep you close to me
but nothing good ever lasts

how old was i
when i first realised
you weren't the person i idolized anymore

i tell you i love you
i tell you that i wish we never met
wishes for the future
may be all that we ever get
but as long as i know you,
 i'll cherish you just like you cherish me

what's wrong with me
what is wrong with me
what's the matter with me
why am i ruining everything
why am i hurting everyone
why is everything ending
because of bullshit i said
that i never needed to

what will happen when i'm gone
will promises remain intact?
or will they wither away,
like the foundation of my very life

crooked paintings on the wall
crumpled, torn notebook pages
of ideas cast aside
the bases of my life spilled out in front of me
where to begin?
where to end

i never thought i'd miss
the ivory colored walls
i've watched darken with age as i've grown up
But the walls are being painted
and i'm leaving soon
where to? i'm not sure
i'm not sure i'm ready

i keep my lights lit
even at night time
these figures in my head
the only things i rely on
i draw lines in the sand
just to watch you all wipe them away

6

My world was spread out in front of me, so thin that holes began to appear in the thin fabric that held the remaining pieces of my life together. My room had already been a mess, but the frantic packing I was doing was making it so much worse. My mind was as foggy as the weather had become. November was approaching fast, and Halloween was just around the corner. I had recently cut my hair short, and I loved how it helped me look less feminine.

Looming over me was my departure date,

the day I would leave my city for a beach town foster home. But, until then, I had Halloween, and I had my life.

It wasn't safe at home. If there was one thing that the social worker was decisive about, it would be that. That's why I was staying with Claire and her family for a while until my dad calmed down and wasn't as dangerous anymore.

I'll never forget what my mom said to the social worker when we were talking about how he could be a potential threat. I've always known my dad to be a dangerous person, his explosive anger partnered with his sheer physical strength and size made him a worthy opponent for people his own size, much less my mother, a petite woman who was several inches shorter than him, and about half of his weight. When he was physically threatening, he was terrifying.

"I'm afraid he's going to come after me, or kill me, or, or set our house on fire." My mother explained shakily to the social worker that day. It was odd seeing her display that kind of emotion, and sure, while it was for herself, it was still shocking to see my emotionally devoid mother show any kind of concern for me, or rather, the house I lived in.

And apparently, he did seem like a threat, and so it was decided, the day the social worker would be visiting him, I would be going to Claire's, and Venus would be going to her friend's house. I'm not quite sure where my mother went, but she probably stayed in a luxury hotel somewhere.

I was packing. How does one fit their entire life into just two bags? Two bags, that was all. I was told that after I came back from Claire's, I would have one more night at home, and then, early in the morning, the social worker would come to transport myself and Venus to, well, god knows where.
As I shoveled clothes and paraphernalia into the bags, I couldn't wonder how things would be if I was born into a different family, and how different my world view would be. I selfishly hoped that maybe, just for once, that Venus could be the subject of ridicule or the target of my father's fury. How different would I be if I hadn't been *abused*? I had never really spoken it out loud, or even really thought the word openly before. It felt so calming to finally think, confidently, that I, Tuesday Ruiz, was a victim of abuse. It wasn't just my parents either, it was Hunter. And yet, that felt harder to admit to myself. Maybe because it's hard to think that someone so young could already be so bad, thinking about how the world has already gotten to and corrupted them. As much as I wish he hadn't, Hunter shaped my life and the image I had of myself more than almost anyone else in my life. How I longed to go back to the time before we met, where the only doubt that I was the most beautiful child in the world came from my parents. And that was what I was, a child. I wasn't even a teenager yet, I was twelve years old.

When I was twelve, I was four feet and nine inches tall. I cut my hair short without caring that I would constantly get called a boy, because I was simply that underdeveloped. And maybe, that was the reason I cut it. I could've been easily mistaken for a boy under ten years of age. And I was twelve when I met Hunter. A middle school relationship turned into a trap, something that I couldn't leave until I was nearly fifteen years old. And at fifteen, I was still a child. I would be a child until I could escape this labyrinth of false and stolen youth that I constantly kept getting deceived with.

I guess the fact that I was abused made it easier for me to be abused again. And Hunter could recognize the signs that I was, too. Hunter was abused, too. I'm not sure that he ever realized it, or if he would ever admit that he knew if he was being abused, but the anger both of his parents displayed whenever he messed up, which was a lot, wasn't normal, and believe me, I would know.

In my observance of the world, I'd discovered that there seem to be two major turn outs for the mentally unhealthy and abused. The first is my case, something fairly straight forward. The abused will ignore the signs of other abusive relationships, and fall into them, again and again, until the weight of constantly healing from torment forces one to introspect and begin to heal the deep rooted trauma, often parental. The second kind of the abused is what I saw in Hunter, and what I tried to fix in him. The abused become the abusive. They learn from their abusers, their tactics and strategies to hurt, and then they use them on other people. These people often aren't bad people, but since they emulate the usually narcissistic behaviors they learned from their abuser, often a parent or someone they've known since childhood, it's easy to think that these people are just that, and sometimes, it can be hard to look past the surface, especially as an abused, and realize that it's just an unfortunate case of too many unfortunate coincidences lining up to create the perfect storm. For some reason, since I was young, these people seemed to flock to me like I was a magnet, and I tried to fix them, often sacrificing bits of myself that I held very near to do what was required of me, or what I thought was required of me.

I sat, jittery in the car as my mother drove me to Claire's house. She lived in an apartment with two of her sisters and her mother and step father. They seemed like nice enough people, at least her mom did. When Claire mentioned to her that I was in danger staying at home, she invited me to stay, and told me I could stay as long as I needed. I'd never had that sense of parental warmth, and I held a sliver of resentment for all those who did.

I had never been the type to stay over at other people's houses. This was the first time I had ever stayed at Claire's, and I didn't really have any other friends . I remember the first time I tried to sleep at someone else's house, I was five years old. It was my kindergarten friend's sixth birthday, and I was delighted to be one of the two people her mom allowed to sleep over. We watched movies and ate snacks before falling asleep far too late for children of our age. I woke up sometime in the middle of the night, una2ble to breath, and I was crying. Her mom rushed to my aid, and needless to say, the experience traumatized five-year-old me, and I didn't try to have a sleepover any time soon after that.

I arrived at Claire's house a warm October evening, and on that particular day, the sky looked like it had been painted with watercolors. The inside was warm, and felt like the comforting thought of family and togetherness, I could've sworn that evening felt like one out of a book. As upset as I was about what was happening and everything I was being forced to deal with, I just couldn't be in a bad mood with Claire. Everything that happened when we were together was so lighthearted, and it seemed almost as though nothing had any consequences, and we were free to do whatever we wanted.

Despite the somberness I had been feeling for the duration of the car ride, when I arrived at Claire's, the same lighthearted theme took over once again. I put the two bags in the room she shared with her sister, and we decided we would be going out until it got dark, since her mom was more relaxed about that kind of thing. We walked a few blocks down to a fancy soft serve ice cream shop, and since the menu was far too confusing for us to understand, we told the person at the counter to just serve us whatever. We ended up being served soft serve ice cream that was swirled with vanilla and orange. I'd always preferred vanilla to any other flavors when it came to sweet things, but this ice cream really showed just why that was. The orange was awful, and Claire and I tried to hide our dislike of it as we made our way to an alleyway behind the building. We danced behind the buildings and played music we vaguely remembered from our childhoods, and I joked about being a runaway and an orphan. I suppose the last bit wasn't really a joke, Child Protective Services had just told me they were taking me away from my parents after all, and isn't that what an orphan is?

Regardless of my parental status, the time that I spent with Claire was meant to be an escape. From both my father and the omnipresent feeling of doom that had been everywhere for me as of late. Though tragedy was the reason for my visit, during the duration of it, I would try to forget about it. But at night, after Claire fell asleep, I would take out my phone and write, write everything. Dumb poetry that had no meaning, concepts for stories I would be embarrassed by in the morning, and every thought that came rushing through my head, it was like the floodgates of my imagination were finally opened, the thoughts like a tsunami that I couldn't push away, and so I wrote.

And the writing caused me to dig. I looked through every single document of writing I had ever produced. I found half finished novels I had written when I was eight, the sentences strung together in broken phrasing like beads. I realized that night how much I missed the person I used to be, the person who could see the best in everyone, who took to broken people, abused people, and tried to make them better, not knowing that it's possible for someone to just be too far gone. Along this path, I found a story I had written at eleven, one so horribly and morbidly dark for a child to write, it left me perplexed, and I began to think about it.

The story was titled *The Kid Who Sleeps in Class* and it was centered around a thirteen year old girl, the oldest of her many siblings, who almost acted as the guardian for her younger siblings. Their mother was dead, and their father was a drunk. I hadn't even written a second chapter, but the stark consistencies with my life, and how realistic the abuse was, showed me how writing had been my coping mechanism far before I even finished elementary school. I began to dissect it.

Why was the mother dead in the story? That one was simple. My mother had never been around when I was younger. She worked far more hours than my father, and I often only saw her or spoke to her once or twice a day. As I got older, I began to notice that as I became more independent, she strayed more, and that once or twice a day turned into once a day, and then once a week. I remember hanging upside-down off the edge of my top bunk in the room that Venus and I used to share, my tears rolling off my face and landing on her Dora the Explorer themed comforter and saying, "I don't think mommy loves us anymore."

I don't think Venus even remembers, she was so young, but Gael used to be such a warm person. If I think back far enough, and forget who she is today, I can remember a mother who used to braid my hair after every bath as I sat on the top part of the sofa and watched *Strawberry Shortcake*, and a mother who always knew my favorite color, even though it changed every other day. It was the gradual pull away from me, the gradual distance she put between us, caring less and less to the point where she didn't remember my birthday or what grade I was in in school anymore that hurt. I know she used to be a good person, I know she used to care about me, so what'd I do to mess it up? What did I do that could possibly be so horrible to make a mother stop loving their child?

Why was the father a drunk? That one was even more simple than the trope about the mother. As long as I had been alive, my father had been addicted to various drugs. His drugs worked differently than alcohol, though. When he smoked, he would calm down, he wouldn't mind as much if I said something or did something wrong. Raphael was different from Gael in the sense that his abuse was more typical. I can say, "my dad hits me", and the police will be on it, they'll step in, and if I have any marks, it's an easy and done case. It's harder to show the emotional marks that Gael made, especially since she prides herself so much on being a savior, saving Venus and I by divorcing our father. The drunkenness was the inability to control himself, and the violence that came when he was sober.

Why did the oldest sister act as a parent for all her younger siblings? Well, I had always felt as though I was parenting Venus more than either of our biological parents, combined, even. Venus would admit this too, she'd told me multiple times how I practically raised her, and when she met Ellio, she jokingly said that he was her new dad.

I began to look deeper, and I found more stories I wrote, dating back to eight years old. It was the same family structure in all of them, dead mother, abusive father that relied on substances, the oldest sibling who was forced to step in to care for the younger sibling or siblings.

So I texted Venus. I didn't need to worry if she was awake or not, Venus was awake at all hours of the night. She was also a writer, maybe less intense than me, but I knew she also used it as a way to express her emotions, as neither of us were very emotional people. And lo and behold, her earlier stories were eerily similar to mine in relation to family structure. Only in those, the youngest sibling was the main character, and they had to deal with always feeling like a burden and unwanted to the older sibling, as well as not having a strong, parental guidance to rely on. Her stories made me cry. I thought about how hard this must have been for Venus, even if she never said it or showed it. We weren't adversaries like our parents wanted us to think, we were siblings, and she was the only one in the world who had any idea what it was like to have my exact parents.

i remember you telling me
when i couldn't have been more than five
that it was normal to fear you
normal to be afraid that you'll follow through

i took the knife from you
and carved my heart out for you
as i lay there, bleeding out with you
i was happy as i handed it to you
because red's your favorite color,
right?

you were a star that shined so bright
 you blinded me
and while i was blinded, you stole my own light,
and left me to die

would you let me waste
some more of your time please?
let me run out the clock,
until the very fabrics of society
come to an end, like us

i said goodnight as the lights went out
the curtains went down,
it was time to go home now
but the energy and spendor
the craving of applause
alas, i could not

it's five in the morning again
and as usual,
i am left alone to cope again

what makes sense anymore
My thoughts certainly don't
But what really does
the color of light?
the shape of water?

when good isn't good enough
and everything tried starts to fail,
the things left are anchors,
sinking me in a perpetual drop
towards whatever

what's beyond the end of today?
the end of the week?
tomorrow?
will a dead star devour us today?
or tomorrow?

when did i become so lost
in your web of lies
that i was unable to make it out

7

I woke up at Claire's house on a hot autumn day, and after the momentary panic I always got whenever I slept over at someone else's house, I was calm. At least I wasn't home, and at that point, anywhere was safer than home, even if it meant sleeping on the couch in Claire's apartment.

To avoid sulking around about my life situation, Claire and I decided it would be best to get out of the house and walk around town. She lived conveniently within walking distance of a neighborhood that was lovely to walk and to shop in.

"Want to buy some cigarettes today?" Claire asked.

"Yeah, for sure. You think I can go in this?" I said as I stared down at my button up and suit pants. There was a shop that sometimes sold cigarettes to minors near Claire's house, but in order for them to sell to you, you had to dress in, well, to put it lightly, revealing clothing.

"No, but I have something you can wear." Claire used to have a white tank top that she wore all the time, that was, before her sister borrowed it and stained it, right in the middle. In order to make it up to her, Claire's sister cut the stained part out in a strip down the center, and used safety pins to hold the shirt together, so the whole middle portion was just an open space. It was far more promiscuous than the clothing I usually wore at that point in my life, but I enjoyed wearing it.

However, while we were walking through her neighborhood, too close to the shop to turn back, I froze. Suddenly, I felt the kind of fear I hadn't felt since I dated Hunter, since, well I hadn't had any reason to have that sort of fear since.

"Oh god." I said, my breath quickening. "Can we sit down?"

"Yeah of course." Claire said without any questioning, and we made our way to a bench at a bus stop. We sat for a moment as I kept myself from slipping into a hysteria.

"I think Ellio is going to be mad at me." I bit my lip to keep it from quivering.

"Why would he be mad at you? He loves you and you haven't done anything." I looked down at the shirt I was wearing, and Claire followed my gaze.

"Is it about the shirt?" She seemed confused. Claire was lucky to have never been in a relationship like the one I had with Hunter.

"He's going to be mad at me because I wore this and this is revealing," I rampled as I was on the verge of tears.

"Do you want to text him right now and ask him?" Claire suggested. "I know that he won't be, but it would make you feel better, you should ask him." Claire reached to put her hand on my shoulder to comfort me, and I flinched before shrugging it away.

Hi Ellio. I typed out, hands shaking.

Hey Tuesday. What's up? He responded nonchalantly.

I wore a kind of revealing shirt today and I'm sorry I didn't ask if you were okay with it first, I can send you a picture of it if you want to see it but it's a tank top held together with safety pins and I'm already out so I can't change. I took a deep breath. The message went from delivered to read, and then he started typing.

Darling, I don't care what you wear and you don't need any sort of permission from me to wear what you want. That would be such a stupid thing for me to be upset over. You should still send me a picture though, because I miss seeing your pretty face. He followed up this message with a heart emoji.

And he was right, of course. Ellio was always right. It was *stupid* for Hunter get mad at me for what I wore, and I was traumatized, from that situation. Yet, paranoia was all that it was.

Once I collected myself, Claire and I made our way to the smoke shop. Like we had anticipated, due to our choices in clothing, the old men at the shop sold us the cigarettes we had gone in for. While in the shop, I remembered that my lighter had recently gone out, and I was in need of a new one. I used the few remaining dollars in cash that I had to purchase one. But on our way to a lawn where we could've smoked, I felt the fear rising like a bubble in my chest yet again.

Ellio was not a fan of the all drinking or the smoking that I used to constantly do during that period, and I was paranoid, again, about how he would feel knowing I bought a lighter. I reminded myself that Ellio would not care, and I convinced myself of it, but I just couldn't shake the general feeling of paranoia that day. I came to realize the reason for this shortly after.

As we were walking back from the store, a loud noise coming from closely behind us caught our attention. One of the people involved in a accident stepped out of an expensive sports car, wearing expensive clothing and sunglasses, and like the ice in my father's heart, I froze. He stood there, across the street, his luxury car completely beat up. And yet, he wasn't staring at the damage done to his car, but at me, and even though his dark sunglasses, I could tell that look was a glare. Claire was looking at me, I was standing stopped like a deer and headlights, petrified of this man who I was supposed to love. I looked at Claire, and before my father could even get back into his car, we started to run.

I don't think I'd ever ran so fast in my life. Despite having comically long legs, months of smoking and various injuries I'd obtained made the already daunting task of running even more difficult.

Yet physical limitations seemed obsolete in that moment, all I could think about was my dad, chasing me, grabbing my neck, suffocating me. And that was enough to keep running.

And I couldn't stop. The hot air turned cold as I began my desperate escape from him. As the adrenaline pumped in my veins, nothing mattered to me anymore. My breath came in short gasps, my eyes shut tight because I could not face the world around me. *This isn't real.* I tried to convince myself by whispering in a pitiful choke. But my heart pounding in my throat assured me otherwise.

"Tuesday!" A voice called my name from what seemed like miles away. I shook it off and kept on, my legs going numb beneath me.

I opened my eyes, and the tears came flooding out, stinging against my face as I continued to run. Eventually, my legs gave out, and I collapsed on a deserted sidewalk, ripping my pants at the knees.

"Tuesday!" Claire shouted, out of breath, catching up to me from several paces up the street.

"How long was he following us?" I said when she caught up, in a tone completely devoid of emotion.

"I don't know. I remember seeing his car a little while back, but I didn't know," She was gasping at the air. "I swear if I knew," She said, shaking her head, "I'm so sorry Tuesday." I stared at the sky.

I lied down, dirtying the white shirt with the grime on the sidewalk. I took the humid air into my burning lungs, my limbs feeling like jelly against the heated pavement.

"Why me?" I said in the same monotone.

"What do you mean?"

"How come all of this is happening to me? I feel like you could write a whole book about just one of my parents, how come both of them had to suck? I don't want to have to go to your house to escape them, I don't want to have to be afraid of them. You don't understand, I would give anything in this would to have them love me back." The look on Claire's face was not one of pity, or sympathy, even. She just looked sad, and what else could I expect from anyone? My stories didn't exactly warrant comforting, especially in the way I told them. Claire said nothing.

I sat up, my head pounding from physical exertion. With the bright sun shining into my eyes and a sky so vibrantly blue it was out of place, I felt like I was falling, almost like I could feel those eighteen miles per second that earth plummets through the universe. Time seemed to slow, and soon, I was deep in my thoughts.

How strange I would have looked to an outsider, a crumpled heap in the middle of the sidewalk staring into the sky for what felt like eternity. By the time I sat up, I could've sworn I felt a chill in the air. I looked at Claire for the first time in what must have been close to an hour. She threw her arms around me in a hug, and I flinched, but this time, I didn't move away. I was too tired for that.

When we arrived at Claire's apartment after our time out, Claire realized she had forgotten to bring a key, and unluckily, her parents weren't home. We tried calling her sister, but she wasn't home either.

"It's okay, we sometimes keep a key under the doormat." She checked the doormat, but there was nothing there. The day just seemed to be getting worse and worse. As we were walking to her backyard to see if one of the back doors had been left unlocked, we noticed that a window on the second story, about 25 feet off of the ground, had been left open. "Okay," Claire said with a smirk. "I know what we can do, but it might sound a little bit crazy."

"I'm listening."

"So we have all this outdoor furniture," She gestured to the lawn chairs and benches that littered her apartment building's communal backyard. "We could stack it all, and if I held it steady, do you think you could climb up and unlock the door from the inside?"

"Yes! That sounds like so much fun." I responded, and we began to stack the furniture.

If there was one thing I learned from that day, it was that we were just specks of dust, if even that, in comparison to all that was going on in our world, our galaxy, the universe. Why not smoke a cigarette? I could never get another chance to. Why spend so much time feeling miserable, wishing I could feel better, if just one or two shots of liquor could do that for me? I deserve to be impulsive, spontaneous, and to just have fun. After all the hell I had been through, why shouldn't I be able to run wild, and to have the privilege of not caring?

After a slightly painful fall through the window, I managed to let Claire inside through the front door.

"Can we drink?" I asked.

"Tuesday, are you crazy? It's two in the afternoon." She looked flabbergasted, I was always so cautious.

"I don't care." I said plainly as I used my phone camera to wipe away the trail of makeup that my tears had left.

"What if my mom comes home when we're drunk? She would kill me. We wouldn't be able to do anything and she would search me and find the cigarettes."

"What if your oven explodes before your mom comes home," Claire looked concerned. "Morbid, I know, but what if your oven explodes, and we die, and we never get the chance to drink again? If we ignore all logic and assume heaven and hell are real, I'm sure I would be deprived of alcohol in hell and would regret not drinking in the moments leading up to my death, would you not?" I reasoned.

"Why don't you think you're going to heaven?"

"What?"

"You said, "I'm sure I would be deprived of alcohol in hell", like you were sure that you wouldn't go to heaven." She turned to face me.

"Well assuming they're real," I looked at her pointedly. "Well, fuck. I don't even know. I guess I just don't consider myself exceptional enough for it. Besides, all of that stuff with sins and things, I just don't think I could make it." I shrugged.

"Interesting." Claire said, and nothing more.

"I don't even believe in it, though. No God that was supposed to be all loving would ever do any of the things that are happening to the world." I paused. "Or me, I guess. I don't think I did anything to deserve this."

"You didn't."

"I know."

"Do you?" I thought about it for a moment. The answer was of course, right? My parents had been shitty to me since I was a toddler, and no toddler is just inherently evil.

Then again, perhaps even just being born was what I did. Without me, my mother would've never married my dad, and so she wouldn't have gotten hurt, and maybe then, she wouldn't have taken it out on me. It was my fault, and I decided that I deserved it.

"Yeah." I lied. "Can we actually drink later tonight? I don't feel like it anymore."

oh, to not exist
to be able to go back
without death
without sorry
but to never be born

i'm not afraid anymore
between worlds and around the stars
i know i'm safe with you

today i realized
i don't remember your phone number anymore
and i felt like i could fly

135

today i realized
i don't remember your phone number anymore
and i felt like i could fly

good morning and goodnight
hello and goodbye
open and close
what do these words have in common?
no clue.

you don't understand
you can't know
because the moment i show you
you'll leave again
and that's okay
cause i would too
but i want you to stay
so you don't get to know

one two three four
please stop banging on my door
five six seven eight
please don't come in, stop it, wait-

let me stay for a while
i've been waiting
i've spent a long time
let me rest for a while

don't remind me
i don't miss you
because though you were horrible
i'm supposed to

i want to know what's out there
the great perhaps, some say
the big maybe
the biggest what if

what's wrong with being wrong
what's bad about doing bad

8

In the car on the way back from Claire's house, I cried. My mother sat there in stunned silence as I did, she had never been good with dealing with me whenever I showed any emotion. I went to Claire's to stay safe, but I left remembering just one more thing I would give the world to stay for. But as I drove home, knowing it would be my last night, I began to think about all the little things I would miss.

The people, mostly. I would miss Claire and Ellio more than anyone. I didn't really have anyone other than that except Venus, and we were promised that we would be kept together, so at least I had her.

Strangely enough, I think I would miss my room. I felt a version of this sadness when, after my parents got divorced, when my father decided to renovate my childhood home to get rid of anything that reminded him of my mother. This included the bedroom I shared with Venus, a small room with built in bookshelves and child sized bunk beds with brightly colored comforters. Our toys and books lined the shelves and were kept in bins underneath our bed, and glow and the dark stars lined the ceiling. Though my childhood room housed some of my worst memories, it held some of my best as well, and I felt the same about my bedroom at the time.

My bedroom was quite large in comparison to the other bedrooms I've had in my life. There was a platform built into the floor of the room that I kept a mattress on, and in the other corner of the room, a small desk piled with torn out notebook pages and half read books I had never quite gotten the motivation to finish. Pressed up against one of the walls was an old, complete collection of encyclopedias that belonged to my great-grandmother. This is one thing that did not change as I moved from house to house in my childhood.

As a young kid with very few friends and hobbies that I was actually interested in, I took it upon myself to read the entire collection. I would sit against the wall for hours and hours trying to force my way through words I still wouldn't understand if I tried to read it now. The collection, which was far too big to pack away in a suitcase, would not be coming with me. I wondered how long it would take for my mother to sell them on Ebay.

When I got home, I couldn't stop staring at my encyclopedias. The navy and gold spines left dusty and untouched for so many years, since it had been so many years since I was disconnected enough to do things that made me genuinely happy. The sun had long gone down when I decided to open one of the encyclopedias again.

It was not long before my tears began to fall onto the yellowed pages of the books. I needed to read these, I had to. Otherwise, in my head, I would've been a failure to my younger self. So I read. If you asked me to repeat anything I learned that night from the encyclopedias, I could not give you an answer. The words were going in through one ear and out of the other, the reading done just to read, not to learn anything like I had wanted when I was younger. Just then, I heard a knock at my door.

I checked the alarm clock on a side table. It was seven in the morning. I hadn't noticed that it had gotten light outside. My mother opened the door.

Being a competitive athlete and model, she always knew she was beautiful. But now, as she stood in my doorway, somewhere between thirty-five and forty years old, without makeup, in sweats and a baggy t-shirt, I could tell that she had aged. The dark circles under her eyes that mimicked mine exactly were our shared genetic trait that let me know that she hadn't been sleeping either. She made eye contact with me for the first time in what had to have been months, but as briefly as the moment had come, it had passed. She looked down at the book in my shaking hands.

"Oh, you're reading the encyclopedias. I remember when you were little, you would read those for hours and tell me about how you wanted to finish them so you could know everything in the world," I looked at the floor, it was strange to be having an actual conversation with my mother, and I wasn't sure how I should be reacting.

"Having trouble sleeping, sweet pea?" She hadn't called me that in years.

"Yeah, I guess." I stared at the book, eyes unmoving. I realized my shoulders were tense.

"Well, I have some good news, and I wanted to tell you in person."

"Yeah?"

"Look at me, Tuesday!" I jumped at her tone of desperation, I had never seen her like that before. I set down the book and shakily looked back up at her.

"Listen. I, okay. I know that I haven't been perfect, or even near that, but I never thought anything I was doing was abuse. I'm not your dad. I'm safe, you can trust me." She caught me looking down. "Tuesday, please. I'm not going to hurt you. Just, I'm sorry. All I want is to fix our relationship, and it looks like there may be more time."

"What do you mean?" I said immediately. More time was all I wanted.

"I just got off the phone with the social worker. It looks like they're backed up and don't think you and Venus are in immediate danger, so they won't be coming for a little bit longer." I felt like a massive weight was lifted off of me. I could see Ellio one more time, I could spend Halloween here, I could finally go to sleep.

She stood like that in the doorway for a while, watching me carefully put away the encyclopedia I was reading away and get into bed, pulling on the comforter she got me when I was ten.

"You still have those stars, huh?" Pointing at the labeled glow in the dark stars she helped me put up when we moved into this house.

"Yeah." I kept trying to steal glances at her without her looking back. "I mean, how would I take them down? They're so high up." I said with a dry laugh, figuring I needed to add something else.

"One second, I need to grab something." She went to the kitchen and returned with a plate of pancakes, my favorite food when I was little. She was trying, I could tell, but it was all too much.

"Thank you, Gael," I managed to say, because what else could I possibly say? She looked down at her feet, and I once again noticed how much she had aged since the last time we had had a real conversation. She looked at me again, and though I refused to look back, I could tell that she meant well and was trying to fix things. "I mean, thank you, mama." I corrected.

"I love you, Tuesday." She choked out before she left in a hurry. I think she was afraid I wouldn't say it back.

★ ☆ ★

Halloween that year was on a Saturday, and lucky for us, it was also daylight savings, meaning I was allowed to stay out an extra hour. Due to the short notice that I would be spending Halloween in my hometown, I barely got the time to make plans with Ellio and Claire. Ellio had already made plans with two of his friends, David and Lucas, but Claire and I were going to meet up with them at a nearby park.

David was Ellio's closest friend. They saw each each other fairly often, and when I started dating Ellio, I became David's friend as well. David looked a lot like the blond guy, Fred, from Scooby Doo. He was very nice as well, almost too nice, actually, sometimes to the point where I became frustrated with jealousy. No matter how hard I tried, I always had an air of coldness about me, and I could never keep calm when I was angry. I was always a timebomb just waiting to explode, jealous of all the nicer people in the world.

Luckily enough, I wouldn't be sober enough to be jealous of how nice David was. In my neighborhood, there was a huge pharmacy that kept the smaller bottles of liquor unlocked, and all the children from the middle schools and middle schools surrounding it would come and steal it. About a month prior, I had gone and stolen a mini bottle of whisky, and I would be damned if Claire, or Ellio, David, or Lucas thought I was going to share it with them.

I arrived at the park earlier than the rest of the people in my group, so I kept on a bench to the side until they came. I was dressed as Lydia from *Beetlejuice*, but no one else who I was going to be hanging out with was going to be dressed up. I didn't mind this, though. I have always used Halloween as an opportunity to be someone you aren't, as cliche as that sounds. I guess this stems from not liking who I was as a younger child, and using every opportunity to take on someone else's personality or being for a night.

Claire arrived at the park shortly after, walking with eyes wide and very, very quickly. She passed by me twice before noticing me.

"Hey Claire?" I said on her second pass.

"Tuuusday!" She called, putting her hand on my shoulders. She had already been drinking, and before the sun even went down too. "I stole like, so much of my mom's alcohol already, tonight is going to be sooo fun!" She stumbled a little bit. "Can I have some of your stuff though?"

"Claire, you definitely don't need any more alcohol," I laughed, "But if I could get some of what you had…" I opened my bottle and took a shot.

Ellio came next. He walked over to the bench Claire and I were sitting on and kissed me.

"I can taste the alcohol on your breath, Tuesday. Just how much have you already drank?" He said, and I allowed myself a laugh. "Can I have some?"

"No!" I yelled playfully, as I shoved the bottle back into the backpack that I brought. I could hear the liquid in the bottle sloshing around in my backpack as my mother was driving, but thankfully, she never paid quite enough attention to me to notice the big things, like my age, so she never noticed the small things, like the sloshing, or if I came home slurring my words just a little bit.

In all honesty, like many of the nights I drank, I don't remember most of it. I don't drink enough every time to completely black out and forget the night, but maybe it's the willingness and want to forget what my life is like for just one night that allows me to truly and fully forget. A trick of the mind, maybe. A placebo.

What I *do* remember was a whirlwind. It isn't often that I'm happy to be out with multiple people, and it basically only happened when I was drunk. By the time Lucas arrived, I had finished a third of the bottle.

"You have whisky?" I remember him asking.

"Yeah, do you want some?" Lucas did not seem like the kind of person to have ever drank before, let alone enjoy it.

"No, I don't like whisky."

Lucas was also very short. Well, that was an exaggeration. He wasn't *too* short, but his reputation preceded him. This being the first time meeting Lucas, (not a great impression, I know), and what I was told was that Lucas was short. This made sense coming from Ellio, though, as he was about four inches taller than me, and Lucas was about three shorter than me. Ellio told me the day afterwards about how I became convinced that

Lucas was a hobbit living in a traffic cone that was nailed to the ground near the play structure. That moment did not highlight my intelligence well.

David lived less than a block away from the park, and had a family birthday, or something like that, so he arrived late. Before he arrived, though, Ellio, Lucas, and I took a trip to his house and talked to him through the bars on his gate.

Apparently, I became convinced those bars were bars to a jail cell, and I became convinced David was in jail. Again, I'm glad I have no memory of this.

About halfway through the night, Claire found some of her friends from middle school and left our group to be with them. I remember them talking about doing some form of hallucinogen sometime during the night, but I don't know if they followed through with it or not. Overall, the escape I had envisioned for the night worked, but at what cost? Far too many people perceived me as a crazy drunk now for my liking. But that's what being young is about, no? Making mistakes, making a fool out of yourself. If it isn't, well, I could at least convince myself that it is, and continue making those choices that would most likely prove detrimental to my future and path that I set myself on, or rather, my parents set me on from a young age. When I was drunk, though, I didn't have to worry about all of the oddities of life. I could just live, free of worry and paranoia. Though this state was temporary, I craved for it all the time, for a few hours to myself to be carefree.

I woke up feeling sick and stupid. Sick because I drank too much, and stupid because I drank to much, and in front of too many people, and because I wasted one of my last nights at home before the government sent me away, or something. My days here were numbered, and I just made myself forget what could've been a happy memory to think back on in ten years, when all of these people forget about me.

Suddenly, a knock that seemed louder than it was sounded at my door. My mother came in.

"Tuesday?" She said, her voice dry and cracking. Her smudged makeup in clear tear tracks.

"What's wrong, mama?"

"They're taking you and Venus away tomorrow." And she began to cry again. With that, she left my room, slamming the door behind her. I sat there, in stunned silence. This was really happening. I called Ellio.

"Ellio? I'm leaving tomorrow. I need to see you today. Can we go on a walk?" Mine and my mother's voices sounded almost identical when we were crying.

they don't love you
they won't love you
i'm the only one
but don't worry
there's only one
person right for you
i'm the one for you

you make loving you so hard
but i'm going to keep trying
i love you? i think

come here and i'll show you
the beauty of the world
but don't get to close
for if you do
that beauty becomes soiled
so watch from afar
if you even dare that
and maybe you'll be here
come morning

i'm trying to get your attention again
i've been working at this since a quarter past ten
and it's getting late and i have school in the
morning
but i want you to tell me you love me

i wish you let me paint my nails when i was young
or let me feel good about myself when i sung
because talking about my childhood makes me
seem depressing

when you aren't woken up in the morning,
or waited for coming home at night,
you have the world to yourself, you can do
whatever.
but do you call it freedom or loneliness?

my gosh
who let these little boys run the world
with their pieces of paper and guns
and why are they so terrifying?

close your mouth and listen
to the beautiful silence

i swear i feel hands all over me all of the time
a gentle touch of nothing that helps me sleep at
night
how could something so invisible just feel so right
i guess i imagine it's you singing a me lullaby

hurry
time is running out
quiet
don't be too loud

9

That day felt like the longest day of my life. It was probably partly due to not sleeping the night before, and also partly because I had a date now, a definite date, of when my life as I knew it would go to hell, and so part of my brain wanted to stretch this day out for as long as possible. It was no use, all days are twenty four hours, and this one was no different, but I could pretend it was.

I thought of my dad again, and I couldn't stop. The thought of him following me kept me awake at night and made me feel sick. And his hands, across my face, around my neck. It was even worse that he wouldn't stop texting and calling me. I didn't have the heart to block him, and I would often wake up to texts either attacking me or apologizing, and I didn't know what was worse.

Other times, it seemed almost like he was completely manipulating me, but could he really do that? He was my father, after all. I didn't know how to respond to any of his messages, because how could I?

You've always had a problem with lying! God, I never want to see you again, I received at five in the morning once.

The moment I read it, I could feel my eyes well up with tears. The fear was back, and so was the pain. Like rubbing salt into fresh wounds. I don't know why this kind of insult never failed to bother me. I guess it's because he's insinuating that something is inherently wrong with me, like I've always been bad, and a liar. It didn't matter that I knew I wasn't lying, when he told me that I was *always* like that, it felt like every time he had said he loved me, every time he had complimented me, like that had *always* been a lie, or like he had been keeping from me how low he really thought of me.

I'm so sorry. I want a relationship with you. I've acted so childish and I hope you can forgive me.

Call me when you can, I love you, he wrote another time.

How in the world was I to respond to that? It felt like my brain was torn into two, to trust him, to not. He told me he loved me, so did Venus. So why couldn't he be like that all the time? Apologize and say he cared instead of making me feel like I didn't matter.

I just totaled my car. I have to go to the hospital but I want to talk to you, it would make me feel so much better.

Now this made me sob. Sure I said I hated him all the time, but I still did care about him. The thought of him getting fatally hurt, or even just hurt, kept me up at night.

Then again, he knew car accidents were a touchy subject for me. It was a secret I kept buried, something I had to work to pull out of the darkest depths of my memory, something not even Claire or Ellio knew about me. But my father did. So why would he use that against me, especially since he was one of the very few people who knew why?

Ellio and I agreed to meet where we had one of our first dates, a big park near his house with lots of secluded places to go to sit down and talk. When I arrived, I felt like my head was somewhere else. It was awful, really. No matter how hard I tried, I just couldn't feel present that day. Ellio made it better, though. When we were together, the time that had slowed to a painstakingly slow rate began to speed up again, and started going fast. Too fast. Soon, these hours would be over, and what would I have left? Nothing at all.

We walked, hand in hand, to a place we had been many times before, a quiet place a little off from the main pathway of the park, under the bridge. We were there for quite a while, and when I finally lifted my head off of Ellio's shoulder and opened my eyes, it was getting dark. As you've probably been able to tell thus far, I'm awful with time, and so after a brief moment of confusion, I turned to face my last sunset in my hometown.

And it was beautiful. The colors of the sky bright and everywhere, like abstract art and my eyes in the sunlight. The orange and pink hues that acted like paint were in contrast with the dark tops of the evergreen trees that seemed to grow everywhere, the sun illuminating Ellio's golden brown hair.

That sunset was so incredibly beautiful, absolutely incomparable to any other natural phenomenon I had ever witnessed. In that moment, the sunset was everything good that I was leaving behind for a small beach town four hours away. It was life, the light being suffocated by the dark in a magnificent, glorious death. The puffy, bruise colored clouds growing darker with age and then beginning to fade, like every bruise I had endured in my fifteen years on this planet, both physical and metaphorical.

I wish that I would've told him how much Ellio meant to me that day, let him know that I would've traded this whole stupid world to just to stay with him there forever, under that bridge and wrapped in his arms. He only knew a fraction of how much he meant to me, how much he had changed my life those past few months, and yet, all I could do was just sit there, watching the light die once again but this time, it felt like it was for me. Like the sunset demonstrated nicely, everything beautiful has to end. And so, eventually, the time came for when I had to go back into the tentative care of my mother again, parked somewhere down the street. I knew it was coming as the sky grew darker, but when texted to let me know, it still felt like my world was collapsing. Ellio and I both looked at my phone, in a melancholic silence, deliberating over what to do next.

"I have to go." I whispered, because even though he knew, I didn't know what else I could have possibly said.

"Really?" He looked into my eyes with a look I could only describe as defeat. And it hurt.

I looked down, down below the bridge to the trail far below. And I looked up, up to where the last bits of color in the sky were finally fading, Icarus having his final hurrahs before plummeting down.

"Can I," It was hard to breath. "Sorry," I squeezed my eyes shut. Maybe if I closed my eyes tight enough, none of this would be real. I could fall back into Ellio's arms again and maybe, just maybe, it would be enough for us to go back in time. Instead of finishing the sentence I so pathetically thought I was strong enough to say, I hugged him tighter.

"It's going to be okay, Tuesday," I could tell he was trying to keep it together for me. "I don't know how we'll get through this but I know we will, I know you will, You're the strongest person I've ever met." I could feel the tears welling in my eyes.

"Can I stay here for another minute?" I asked, muffled because my face was pressed into his shoulder. I was afraid that if I looked at him, I wouldn't be able to stop myself from doing something embarrassing.

"Of course. I love you so much."

But at the end of the day, nothing is permanent. Not my childhood home, people, or this hug. And so I had to let go. I still couldn't look at him. The tears were far too close to brimming for me to even consider looking at him in the eyes.

"You have no idea how much I'm going to miss you." He said softly.

"No, I definitely will, because I'm going to miss you more."

I guess I was tired enough after my day of mourning my life in my city to fall asleep as soon as I got home. Unfortunately for me, I awoke in a cold sweat shortly after six in the morning in a cold sweat, face sticky from tears. Unable to think of another solution, I called Ellio.

"Hello?" He mumbled, confused and tired from being just woken up.

"Ellio, hi. I had a bad dream and I need to talk to you right now."

"Tuesday," He said clearer, suddenly at least ten times more awake. "I'm here, it's okay. Do you want to talk about it?"

"In the dream, I knew I was going to die at midnight, and we were on the phone, and suddenly, at around eleven thirty, you said, "okay, I'm tired and going to sleep now!", and left me all alone, and then, when I died, I became a ghost, and I was crying and trying to get my mom's attention, but she didn't notice me because I was dead." After the initial shock of waking up from this, I realized this wasn't as bad as I had made it out to be. "Sorry, that was stupid. It just felt so real and I called you because I was panicking and didn't know what else to do. You should go back to sleep."

"You're crazy if you think I'm going back to sleep before you do." He chuckled softly. "I love you."

"I love you, but I don't think I can get back to sleep. Besides, I only have," I checked the time.

"About five hours before I have to leave, I might as well make use of it." I realized I had been pacing and slumped against the wall.

"You're impossible," He joked. "But fine. I'll go to sleep. I'll text you in the morning, and can you call me when you can? Like, when you get there? Because I already miss you so much and can't wait to hear your voice again."

"Yes of course. Now, go to sleep. I love you."

"I love you."And he went to sleep.

I didn't quite know what to do with my last few hours, and so I stared at the wall. As I looked around at what used to be my safe place, I realized that this, this was never home. Sure, it was where I lived, and where I would come to be alone whenever things got bad for me, but comfort and safety aside, I didn't really see the sentimental value I had placed on it just nights before. I don't think I would miss my room. The safety it provided, yes, but the memories I could do without.

As I walked around this room that was my refuge for the duration of middle school and high school, I felt my pain for leaving it obliviated. It was a bittersweet feeling, realizing that I no longer needed my safe haven, and that I grew out of it, just like all the other things here.

Expect for Ellio and Claire. But I wasn't prepared to feel that kind of grief, and so I pushed it aside for some time. I continued to pace, my boredom exasperating. Then it dawned on me, the encyclopedias.

Yes, there would always be things I never knew. Words I will never be able to define and stories that I just can't get the message of. That was okay, though. Who knows when I could die, it could be tomorrow or in a hundred years. So why waste time worrying about it? If I die tomorrow, I would rather have spent my life reading my encyclopedias instead of worrying about not finishing them. So naturally, I read. I wouldn't get far before I had to leave, or past the "D" section, but I now know what dacryocystitis is, as well as what death tics are. And those are just two more things I might've never known if I had kept worrying.

Even though I was checking the clock every few minutes, morning came far too quick for my liking. Before I knew it, Venus and I were sitting on the curb, waiting to be picked up by a social worker.

"I can't believe we're really leaving," She said, nudging a pebble in our driveway with her platform shoes. "I don't know, I've never lived anywhere else, and I'm just kind of afraid, are you?" I thought about it for a minute.

"No, I don't think so." I said hesitantly.

"What about Ellio? And mama, and everyone else. Are you not going to miss them?" She looked at me.

"Of course I'll miss them!" I returned her gaze. "But at the same time, this is happening because it's meant to, because, well, I don't know! God says so, it's in the stars, the universe, hold on, I'll be right back."

I ran back inside with just minutes left before we were to leave. I grabbed a chair from the dining room and stood on it so I could collect my glow in the dark stars. I had always had them on my ceiling, no matter where I lived, so you could bet that, wherever I was going, they would be on that ceiling. I had almost made it out when a quiet voice stopped me at the door.

"Tuesday?" My mother asked, eyes red from crying.

"Hi Mama." We hadn't yet spoken that morning.

"Sweet pea, come here," She said as she opened her arms. Unable to contain myself, I ran into them. "I know you're going to take care of Venus,"

"Of course." I interrupted.

"But I just need you to promise me that you'll take care of yourself, too." She stepped back and held my face, I was crying again. "We were all put on this earth for a purpose, and you, Tuesday, are special. You are going to do amazing, incredible things someday."

"I promise. But, mama?"

"Yeah?"

"Can you also promise me that you'll take care of yourself?" Just then, a car honked from outside.

"Of course," She looked at the floor. "You better get going, I don't want them to wait. I love you. And tell your sister I love her, too."

"I love you!" I called as I ran out and down to the waiting social worker.

And with that, Venus and I left. We arrived at a hotel four and a half hours later. The weather in this beach town was cold and rainy, and there was a storm in the forecast for later that evening. I couldn't wait for night so I could sneak out.

when i was younger,
i thought that only happy stories could be good
but then i learned the beauty of the bittersweet
and the deliciousness of the sad

maybe it's possible to forgive
everything you've made me go through
because maybe inside
you need to forgive too

everything truly good
hurts a little at first

I think i'm happy
light as a feather
floating high above the world
unstoppable
what could go wrong?

i wish i could
make myself go to sleep
before four o'clock in the morning
but night is always when i am my best
so why stifle creativity for a few extra hours

sorry, i don't think
i'm sorry anymore

i wish the world would just be quiet

it's already getting better
i didn't believe it at first
but just wait
just wait
because it's already happening

my favorite number now is nine
as in september
as in the ninth
as in o'clock
maybe because it's shaped like a balloon
reaching upwards
towards the sky

a bittersweet sense of relief
as in now i don't have to suffer
but to grieve

a bittersweet sense of relief
as in now i don't have to suffer
but to grieve

10

The waves broke from the surface of the ocean and ran, daring, uncontrollably. Like a dangerous, navy and white horse, breaking free from the mass of water and coming down, hard, against the rocky shore.

Maybe a horse isn't the best analogy, though. Horses can be trained, but the ocean is ruthless, untameable. I wrapped my trench coat tighter around me, uselessly attempting to keep myself dry, the dark, heavy drops raining down on me like bullets. I looked out across the raging sea, because what else was I supposed to do? There was not much to do up in the lighthouse.

I was not going to go back to that hotel. That place was full of misery and pain disguised as hope, I would have rather thrown myself over the railings of this lighthouse than spent another minute there.

That was the hill I would die on. I slumped to the concrete floor.

I couldn't run away, though I hated this place more than anywhere. Venus would be here all alone, and if I contacted her at all, I would be able to be found, and I don't think I could live without Venus. I already put her here, this was already my fault.

But wasn't everything? For the past few months, or even my whole life, wasn't it all my fault? I was the one who created this fucked up family in the first place, I was the star. It all centered around me. In this situation, it was my fault. I only had three years left. I could've waited to call the authorities. I would've been okay, right? Then again, he tried to kill me. What if he got sick of me, or Venus? I didn't want to think about it. My thoughts tore at each other and fought like the writhing sea below me, slamming itself against the jagged shoreline.

I reached into my coat pocket, hands numb with cold, and drew out an old notepad and a pen. I tapped the pen against my leg as I listened to the wind howl, a kind of chaotic peace, a hauntingly beautiful song. How I loved the rain. Under different circumstances, this would've been the perfect working environment for me, but in the current, I simply could not get my mind to relax. And like I always do when I'm trying to reign in my ideas, I wrote.

I was far too shaken to write anything of meaning, and so I decided I would write an alternate ending to *The Man in the Meadow*. It went like this:

It was four thirty in the morning, and the man was still in the meadow. The sky had already begun it's lift from the impenetrable darkness he had cast upon the world. Soon, the sky would lighten to his brightest, and the birds would begin to sing to break the night. It was warm, it was July. If the man closed his eyes, and thought hard enough, he could very well pretend that he was a young boy, still grasping his mother. Oh, what he would have given to be young again. Her long dresses, her soft hair. Soon, mother. He thought. It won't be long now, he assured her in his mind, and it wasn't going to be. He was so very tired.

When he heard the first bird begin to sing, he stood up and began walking through the meadow towards the other side, because strangely, in all his years in this town, he had never been to the other side of the meadow. Looking out at it's vast expanses was enough for the man while he lived. Now, it was not, at least, not anymore. He began to walk, and walk, and walk.

Soon, the sky had painted himself a dark aquamarine, and the scent of summer began to sprout from the poppies and wildflowers. Heat began to rise, the day had almost begun.

Perhaps the man would have made it to see what was on the other side if he had been younger, his limbs wouldn't feel as stiff as the tree roots that dug deep under their tiny town, and he wouldn't have been weakened by the arthritis that had plagued him for the last years of his life. Nevertheless, he had made it surprisingly far for a man of his age and stature, but somewhere along the journey, the man simply had to stop. He wasn't the same young man he had been years ago.

And so, the man lay down in the meadow one last time, he lay down, and despite the heat, it began to rain. Dense, heavy droplets fell from the aquamarine sky himself, cascading down the man's face, covering the man's universe in a haze, and his eyes began to blur.

On closer inspection, it was not raining from the sky, but from the man's eyes, cloudy with cataracts. And yet; it seemed as if both the clouds in the sky and the clouds in his eyes sensed the man in all of his anguish, and began to cry with him.

It won't be long now, mother. He told himself once again. It wasn't going to be.

Perhaps things would be different if the man had been born wealthy, or handsome, or anyone besides himself. Perhaps if he had only... The what if's were all gone now, because they were just that; what if's. Not real, and it was far too late to change anything.

Drenched in his own tears and the tears he seemed to have manifested from the sky, the man rested his head, and reached into his coat, producing a sprig of lavender. He tucked it behind his ear, he closed his eyes.

In the back of his mind, the sky seemed to turn dark again, then it was bright, and then the sky turned into a beautiful shade of lavender, like his mother's dresses, like his mother's perfume, his mother was everywhere and nowhere, everything and nothing, and yet... I digress; it continued to rain those swollen raindrops, and with the sun steadily rising in the east, it was all a beautiful mess. A beautiful, beautiful mess, and it reminded the man of the very meadow he was in. His so dearly beloved meadow. This was heaven, this was it. The man was so very nearly content, the man had almost all he needed.

But alas, he would never get the only thing he wished for in that moment. His mother was no more, and any moment now, he would be too. To be no more is to simply be no more, and so he was stuck. The man was stuck, so close to having everything. Imprisoned in this beautiful mess that is life, this perpetual, never ending cycle of men, women, and children living and dying, and having no impact on the world. And so, we live on; hoping and praying that tomorrow, it will all be better; tomorrow it will be okay. Life, this beautiful mess, will remain a mess, and perhaps, just maybe, it can even remain beautiful. But that doesn't matter, at least not to the man, because the man, and his worries, his fears and regrets, they were all gone.

Though the temperature surely was edging freezing at this point, I yearned for those summer days long ago when I would eat sticky popsicles on my back deck with my cousins, and the sun heating up the artificial wood beneath our bare feet. Then again, wasn't that happiness all artificial as well? The fun made up, manufactured by the adults in our lives to control us.

If we think this way, isn't everything made up? Every experience I've ever had has been orchestrated by something or someone, I'm in control of nothing.

There's good in the world, though. Even if everything is out of my control and tainted with other people's orchestration, I know that there's good, because I know Ellio. A thunderstorm in a world of uncertainty and drought, a single ray of sunshine coming through the branches of a tightly packed forest. Just good, and a kind of good that is completely unmanufactured and real. There wasn't much to do in a lighthouse during a storm, so I looked out across the sea, determined to spot a boat, or some sort of animal.

Eventually, I did.

Far out, so small I wasn't sure if I even saw it at first, was a tiny fishing boat, being thrown every which way due to the storm. In the boat, a lone fisher, desperate to make their way to the shore in their fragile boat.

And I became captivated. How does one not?

As the spec of their boat grew larger in the angry sea, it seemed as though they were making their way, slowly, but steadily, towards the shore, towards the light. The rain came down harder still, and the wind picked up it's pace, but still, I was clinging to the railing of the lighthouse, knuckles turning white.

To this person, my problems about where I was living didn't matter. All that mattered was that I was, well, living.

And if.

If they can make it through the storm.

If they can find their way home.

And if they can find home, maybe, one day, once this all clears up, Venus and I can find home, too. Maybe that's our home with our mother, maybe she can get better, maybe she can prove that she can be a capable parent. Maybe my father can learn to forgive me, or maybe, I can learn to forgive him.

Like I had told Venus before we left, Everything happens for a reason. The universe had a very mysterious way of working, and for some odd reason, it decided that this would happen, and that's okay. I knew Venus and I would be okay.

And so I stared out into the beautiful mess of the world, hoping the maybe's of today would somehow turn into the yes's of tomorrow.

as winter came to an end
and flowers began to bloom
the happiness i felt with the cold
was whisked away on a breath of spring
and i had to learn how to love
the pain of sun again

two years ago i would've never imagined
that there would be a wall between us
but maybe the hardest walls to walk through are
doors
uncertainty pushing me back into the cage i built
around myself

the feeling of regret i get
when i know i've messed up my life again
is more of a friend
than i've ever had

and in that other life,
we would still say
"in another life"

i would stay up all night
even if it just meant you'd
get two hours of sleep
instead of one

home doesn't feel like home anymore
i've found somewhere else
a place that doesn't even exist
yet it still feels more like home than here
how strange

no one will notice,
i said as i stole a cookie from the jar
no one will notice,
i said as i ran out and away

i may die
my time come too soon
my life flashing before my eyes
but when i do
at least i wrote it beautifully

the last time we met
we were smiling,
and we said goodbye
like we were going to say hello again.

i wonder why goodbyes are good
because there's nothing good about them
they seem like one of those little things
us humans like to say to make ourselves
feel better

we both know there's no good in losing something
good
but i'll say goodbye to you anyway,
because you were so good

adieu

ABOUT THE AUTHOR

Amara Romero is an author, poet, and student from Oakland, California. They are the author of the novella, *Tha Wanderlust That Will Not Let Me Be*. Amara lives at home with their mother and sister, along with their wonderful goldendoodle Roxy. A lfielong lover of literature, their favorite books are *Looking for Alaska* by John Green and *The Great Gatsby* by F. Scott Fitzgerald.